I know
you are
but
What am I?

Heather Birrell

Andrew! I know what you are, but... Oh dear. Too little sleep and two glasses of pub wine. Thank you for reading and speaking for my students. Heather Dec 13 2012

Coach House Books

first edition

Published with the assistance of the Canada Council for the Arts and the
Ontario Arts Council. The publisher also acknowledges the Government
of Ontario through the Ontario Book Publishing Tax Credit Program and
the Government of Canada through the Book Publishing Industry
Development Program.

NATIONAL LIBRARY OF CANADA CATALOGUING IN PUBLICATION

Birrell, Heather, 1971-
    I know you are but what am I? / Heather Birrell. – 1st ed.

Short stories.
ISBN 1-55245-139-9

    I. Title.

PS8553.I792156 2004   C813'.54   C2004-902055-2

Very funny,
but how would you like it
if you never knew from one day to the next
if you were going to spend it

striding around like a vivid god,
your shoulders in the clouds,
or sitting down there amidst the wallpaper,
staring straight ahead with your little plastic face?
          – Billy Collins, from 'Some Days'

But what we can't say, we can't say
And we can't whistle it either
          – F. P. Ramsay

CONTENTS

THE GOLDEN HOUR

My brother Carl was hit by a train and survived!

The doctors say it's a miracle and want to write it up in their medical journals. He was out in BC somewhere pretty remote, walking across a field with his buddies (and yes, they'd had a few beers, maybe a joint). He decided to walk along the tracks and he didn't hear the train coming (and yes, his ears are fine). One of his friends saw the train, sprinted across the distance, grabbed Carl and tried to pull him back. Still, the train hit them both and ... they both survived!

This is the story Marion tells the convict on the bus to Buffalo. Of course, at the time she tells the story, she does not know he is a convict. If she had known, she might have chosen another story, or told the story differently, with her eyes less wide. She does not tell him that Carl sometimes forgets where the door to his room is, or that he can now do sums in his head Marion has difficulty with on paper. These are details that float like tiny bits of fluff; they get up your nose or trouble your vision. What is clean and true about the story is the train – its force and momentum – and Carl, oblivious.

'Yeah, I was in BC once. Riding with a bunch of guys in the Rock Machine, from Quebec. You heard of those guys?'

'Yeah. I think they blew up some people outside of Montreal.' Marion is heedful of her words, but not too heedful. She suspects her seatmate of bluster. 'Do you live in Buffalo?'

'Well, sort of. Gotta go back to jail.'

'Oh.' Marion is having an affair with a married man named Gene. Gene believes she is too prone to conversation, that it will get her into trouble one day.

'Don't believe me, huh?' He pulls a laminated card from his wallet. 'Here.'

'Okay,' says Marion, taking the card. It is a prison ID card, neat and numbered. 'Well, okay.' Is it rude to ask what he's in for?

'I got kids, y'know. And I'm a nice guy. I mean, I visit them, tell them stories. In the morning I get up, play a little guitar. I love my kids.'

Marion knows that he does, the same way she knew he would choose her when she saw him outside the Pizza Shack in Albany, *Marlene* emblazoned on his bare shoulder above a roaring red jungle cat.

When she boarded in Brattleboro, Vermont, the bus had been nearly empty. Two kids in rainbow hats sat in the navy blue recliners, heads jigging, all plugged up with earphones. She chose a seat towards the back, next to a window, and raised a hand to Gene, who was leaning against his car, craning a little to locate her. They had spent the weekend in the woods, talking and grappling benignly by the fireplace. Gene had moved to New York City for a few months to work on a fast-paced, gritty TV series. Most of the scenes were to be shot back home, in Toronto, but there were some things – the soot and swagger – that Canadians could not emulate. Gene was a cameraman with an idea for a screenplay.

'So, we have a holdup in a café, or maybe a bar, although I don't want this to get too saloon-like, and when the holdup guy leaves, he says, *No one make a move, because my accomplice is here, among you.* Well, maybe not *among you,* that sounds a little biblical, but you know what I mean … It's understood that if someone sets off an alarm, calls 9 1 1, whatever, the accomplice will do something. The catch is that when the accomplice finally gets up to leave, he says the exact same thing – that his or her accomplice is now the watchdog. Everyone suspects everyone. Along the way we have little vignettes, little windows into the lives of the people in the café-slash-bar … ' Gene sighs exuberantly at this – the inventiveness, the volatility. Gene sighs like no one else Marion knows, as if he is shrugging off a sweaty monster of a knapsack. Something about his sighing makes her want to hit him then hug him.

'And if anything were to happen, the accomplice does what? The threat has to be real for there to be actual tension.' They are sprawled like sultans by the hearth. Marion keeps her eyes trained on the flames as she speaks.

'Good point,' says Gene, and pokes at the blue centre of the fire. 'Good point,' he says again, reflectively, encouragingly.

Marion tries to suppress it, the way her blood always rises to the tender turf around her ears when Gene endorses her. 'It's all suspense and no resolution. Everyone is an accomplice? That's life, not movies. Who wants life?'

'Yeah, too many far-reaching implications … ' The fire is dying down. Gene moves closer to Marion, then kisses her.

Sunday, Gene managed to find a sushi bar in a nearby town. The sashimi sat like fancy paperweights on the red tablecloth between them, and Gene told stories about starlets on famous film sets he had worked on, or his neurotic dog. Marion listened, her breaths coming too quickly, like a starlet on a famous film set, or a neurotic dog. There was a clump of white on Gene's lapel, a starchy corsage of mismanaged rice. He was not couth, Gene, or even that comely, but he was brave. Last month he had surprised her with a weekend in Stratford; they spent two nights there while his wife, Joyce, visited her mother in Ottawa. The bed and breakfast had dark wood panelling in the dining room, and a large four-poster bed which made Marion feel unworthy and pampered at once. On the walls were old playbills in walnut frames and a small sketch of Anne Hathaway's cottage in the real Stratford in England. Marion loved the sketch for its tininess and fine scratchy lines and would often study it while Gene was in the bathroom at the end of the well-carpeted hall.

That weekend, Gene rented a tandem bicycle and they rode along the river, stopping to throw the swans balled-up bits of bread. It was on one of these stops that Marion had asked Gene about Joyce, whether she minded that he was not with her in Ottawa. Gene steered the bicycle off the path so they could coast down towards the river bank. Marion found herself pedalling uselessly while gripping her immobilized handlebars. The sun was sinking, mottling the sky with pink, pot-bellied clouds. Gene climbed off the bike and bent to examine a patch of wildflowers growing out of an abandoned garbage can.

'Joyce is a very capable woman. She can manage on her own.' He threw his voice out across the water, skipped it like a flat stone along the shoreline. 'Who's Anne Hathaway, anyhow?'

'Um, she was Shakespeare's girlfriend.'

'Oh.' He turned and walked towards her, squelching purposefully along the bank. 'I love you, Marion.'

'I love you, I love you, I love you,' Marion said. She had become the type of woman who used the word *love* like salt, to heighten the taste of things.

Gene hadn't wanted her to take the bus. 'I think you'll find the quality of people much better on the train.'

Marion stares at the convict's scrubby moustache.

'I'm Randy. You are – ?'

'Renée. Renée Ellsworth.' She uses her soap opera alias.

'Hey, Renée. Aren't you gonna ask me what I was in for?' He stretches in his seat.

She nods but does not actually ask.

'Drugs. The first time, anyway. Then when I got out, on parole, y'know, I'm in this bar, and there's the guy that turned me in, just sitting there, pleased as pie. And I had to say something. Wouldn't you?'

Marion nods again and pulls her finger across the window in the shape of a sideways figure eight. Infinity. But the glass is too clean and dry; what's left is the ghost of a smudge. Across the aisle an old man is muttering unpleasantly about Holy Scripture.

Back in Toronto, Marion is an art teacher at an alternative high school. In the yard, the kids lower their eyelids like venetian blinds when she walks by, surmise their situations through the slits. Marion thinks they like her, in a noncommittal, egalitarian sort of way. In the classroom, they blink and blithely call her by her first name, arch their eyebrows only slightly when she suggests a brush stroke or lectures on colour and form.

Most of them sketch large, abstract egg shapes, and sometimes spirals, then grit their teeth as they throw the colours onto the canvas. One of them, the smallest, Sacha, smiles at her often, and paints only in purple. Sometimes she stays to help rinse the brushes. Marion stands over one of the large sinks watching the colours swirl away as Sacha explains to her how little time they have, really, to clean the air, the water, the sky. When Marion looks up from the swirling she is always surprised at the degree of sadness in Sacha's eyes. It is more textured and stoic than the despair of adolescence; it scares her in a way she cannot name. There is a passive resistance in Sacha that emerges startlingly, in flashes of orange on the canvas, or in unconscious gestures of concentration. But sometimes, if the barometric pressure has risen or the planets are not properly aligned, she raises her voice. *Mi-iss.* Two syllables, the second soaring in thin complaint. *Mi-iss, he's really disturbing me.* And Marion sends them out in the hallway to resolve their differences. To negotiate a settlement.

The bus careens slightly, then rights itself.

'Wouldn't you have to say something?' Randy stretches again, so that his long legs jostle Marion's; this is bossy, not sexy.

Marion ponders boundaries, but also feels blessed. When she talks to Gene next, she will anticipate his *I told you so.* She will dazzle him with droll, self-deprecating description. She nods at Randy.

'So, there was a brawl. He comes at me with a broken bottle, was gonna slit my throat. I grabbed a chair, smashed it across his head. He fell against the bar. Out cold. They carried him out on a stretcher.'

There is a prompt required of Marion. 'And?'

'Was in a coma for two months, then he died. Just gave up the ghost. Lucky for me the judge understood it was self-defence. I mean, a broken bottle, for fuck's sakes.'

From Brattleboro to Springfield, Massachusetts, Marion had counted twelve new passengers. The seat beside her remained empty; the view out the window hilly, busy with white church spires. But in Albany, Randy was waiting. When she stepped down from the bus, there he was, cigarette snuggled in the V of his fingers, one leg propped up on a cement planter. In the food court, the light made Marion blink and tear up and want a doughnut. She stood in line. Back outside, Randy's cigarette smelled good, bracing and woodsy. She bummed one.

And then she had found herself telling Carl's story, thieving it really, trying to make it her own. What she wanted to convey was not only the improbability (hit by a train, for God's sakes!), but also her place in the narrative. *You must understand*, she wanted to say, *you must understand, this is my brother we're talking about here.*

On the tiny TVs that hang above their heads, a movie is playing. In the movie, a band of angels is fighting a gang of vampires on some city's mean streets. Randy leans towards Marion as they whiz along the highway.

'You know what my son said when I told him I was sorry but I'd have to go away for a while? He said, "You're not sorry, you don't hurt people if you're sorry." Kind of got things back to front. But I see him sometimes now – he's a teenager, big lug of a guy. My wife left me, though. She's with some boy toy she met at the Legion. Came and visited me for twelve fucking years, then as soon as I get out on parole, good behaviour, she's off to the races. You married?'

'No, I was engaged once, though. Just didn't work out. He was too, I dunno, just too ...'

Randy is looking at her closely. 'Yeah, too ... I know.' He puts his walkman on, turns up the sound. 'Bruce Springsteen,' he says to the ceiling.

Marion knows some Bruce Springsteen songs. *Hey little girl, is your daddy home, did he go away and leave you all alone? Whoa-oh, I got a bad desire. Born in the USA-ay.*

Marion's mother lives in the USA, with her new husband. Marion hasn't seen her real father for twenty-four years. He could live in the USA. He could live anywhere he wanted. Marion's mother says the only real difference between Canadians and Americans is that Canadians believe there is a difference between Canadians and Americans. But Marion does not agree.

'Space, Ma, it's all about space. Fahrenheit and guns. It's a different mentality. We've grown up in the shadow of a super-power. That can't help but influence us.'

Marion's mother harrumphed. 'Right. Well, fat lot of good all that shadowy space has done us, eh?'

The bus pulls into another roadside food court, and Marion is glad. She is hungry, and has had to pee for a long time, but was alternately irked and exhausted by the prospect of pushing past Randy's black-denimed knees. In the small entranceway, he stops to look through the glass into the dining area. Some of the passengers from the bus already have their food; it sits in tidy packages on the chunky green tables.

'I could really use a coffee,' Randy says, opening the door for her. Next to two posters of missing children and one of a wanted criminal, a boy in brown dungarees traipses through a booth of brightly coloured plastic balls.

'That's the play area,' he adds.

In the bathroom, a woman is standing with her legs crossed, supporting herself against a stroller. She looks Marion up and down, makes a decision.

'Can you watch him for a minute, please? I really have to go.'

The woman is wearing a crop top and tight jeans. The exposed portion of her tummy trembles as she speaks.

Marion nods, and the woman disappears into a stall. The baby is sleeping, one angry fist clenched by his cheek. Lambs in sunglasses leap across his T-shirt. Marion reaches down to touch one of them. The woman steps out of the stall.

'Thank you so much. I was dying.' She zips her jeans, does the snap, all with one hand.

'You're welcome. He's really sweet.' Marion has a sudden impulse to scoop up both mother and child, one under each arm, and haul them around with her, as proof. Proof of what? She wants to say survival, trust, something sinewy that lasts. But she does not say anything, she only thinks these things, in a provisional, embarrassed way, and waves hastily to the woman as the bathroom door swings shut behind her.

Back in the bus, Randy is talking again.

'So, I'm in this work program now, got a job at a garage, mostly I fix bikes. Thing is, I gotta live with my sister in Albany, and she's a real holy roller. Won't even let me watch the wrestling. I have it on pretty good authority that her husband's gonna leave her, he's not into all that Christian shit. Anyway, my sister, Janie, she's put this curfew on me, locks the door after nine p.m. Makes it hard to have any fun.'

'I have a sister like that. Her name's Yvonne. She lives in Vancouver.'

Yvonne worries about Carl and Marion. Marion because she is thirty-one years old, single and somewhat surprised by this. Carl because he is twenty-eight years old, jobless and happy.

Carl had been visiting Yvonne when he got hit by the train. He called Marion the day before the accident. She could tell by the pleasant, semi-strangled sound of his voice that he was high.

'Listen to this, Mare.' She could hear him rummaging in the fridge. 'The chickens have access to outside pastures and feed on the natural ground cover and other flora and fauna.' He cleared his throat. 'It's on the egg carton. Big as anything, right on the front.'

Marion called Yvonne before she left for Vermont.

'How's Gene?' Yvonne said.

'It's like a game,' Marion had replied.

There was a game they used to play at grade-school birthday parties. The object was to pass an orange along to the next person, clutching it between your chin and your chest. If you dropped the orange or cheated with your hands, you were disqualified. Boy, girl, boy, girl, went the line. It was less of a game, really, than a manoeuvre; a manoeuvre that forced you to contort and sidle up close to someone.

'You're smoking again, aren't you?' Yvonne put down the phone to hoist the baby to the other hip. Cam was four months old and perfect, his face a plate of carefully arranged gourmet features, his small body pink and poised for growth.

'How's Cam?'

'You've got to find a relationship where there isn't so much darn strategy involved.'

But that's the part I like. Marion pictured Yvonne's sandalled feet, the dried flowers hanging on the wall next to the framed photograph of her partner, Gil. She looked around her own apartment. She had painted the walls a glossy aubergine when she moved in, with the hope that the sheen and luxuriance would make her feel more sleek and healthy than she actually was. Instead, the walls made the room seem dim and pretentious, as if they were sneering at Marion's inexpensive bamboo furniture. It was a terrible match. She wondered if eggplants even grew on the same continent as bamboo. It occurred to her that she didn't know where bamboo grew, and this seemed to her a huge, perhaps unbridgeable, gap in her fund of useful lore.

'Yvonne, does Gil know anything about trees and plants or does he just stick to creatures of the deep?'

'Of course he does. We're all part of the same giant, interconnected ecosystem, you know.'

Gil is a marine biologist, a career path he chose, Marion believes, simply because sometimes it is easier to become the stuff of schoolboy chants than to spend your entire life railing against them. *Gil the fish face*, the kids used to call him, in a singsong, as he floundered on the sidelines of the playground, Yvonne has explained to Marion in hushed, empathetic tones. Gil is the sort of man Marion would never allow herself to fall in love with;

his eyes are too ample. They're frightening, like oceans or trash compactors. Things you cannot see to the bottom of.

Randy coughs conspiratorially. 'Thing is, my social worker, she's a nice lady and all, but she keeps emphasizing the importance of family. What she doesn't understand is that my sister is a fucking bitch, excuse my language. I guess it's good I got a roof for now, and only back to the prison every coupla weeks to check in. I guess that's the good part.'

Yvonne is a social worker. Mostly she works with troubled children. She tells Marion stories. Like the one about the seven-year-old who put his mother's cat in a pillowcase and smashed it against the wall until it stopped mewling.

'You know what that means, when the signs are so clear, so early?'

'No more pets?' said Marion hopefully.

'No.' Yvonne paused. 'Psychopath.'

It used to be, when they were kids, that Marion was the smart one. Or maybe she was just lazy, with a good vocabulary.

'We'll play Cloak,' she would say to Yvonne, and drape herself over her sister's shoulders so that her arms hung down in front. 'You get to wear me all day.'

'All day?'

'Unless you can undo the secret antique clasp.' Marion would lace her fingers together, tightly, and not let go.

'You got a boyfriend, though, don't you? I can usually tell. Something about your eyes or something. Sometimes I don't get it, though. There's this girl, she works at the gas station next to the garage, young, maybe even a bit younger than you. I thought she had a boyfriend. You're not that young, though, are you? How old are you?'

'Twenty-nine,' says Marion, jealous of the gas-station girl. Jealous of the gas-station girl?

'So, we been out on a coupla dates. She's the first person I ever told about when the guy, the guy who turned me in, was in a coma, how it felt, waiting all that time. That it was a relief, really, when he died. The waiting's always the hardest part.'

'Carl was in a coma for two days after the train hit him.' Marion has to shout over the revving and rooting of the bus.

'So we got something in common, then,' Randy shouts back. 'Besides this stinkin' bus.'

Marion sniffs. She doesn't mind the bus so much, although she can see the trip has begun to wear on some of the passengers, who appear torn between the desire to nap and the fierce feline need for a stretch. The old man across the aisle is sleeping in short staccato sentences, his head jerking definitively upwards every few minutes. The bus slows and then stops in Syracuse, where three college kids in leather jackets board, cursing and chortling under their breaths. Marion is not tired, although she does feel relaxed and benevolent, and curious in an unfocused sort of way. There is a small zigzag of a scar just above Randy's temple.

'What's it like, you know, on the inside?' Ungainly question, but she indulges herself.

'Fine. I just kept to myself, didn't get involved in anything, played my guitar. More waiting. Got pretty good at Scrabble, though.'

He played Scrabble, Gene, Scrabble! Marion can hear herself exclaiming, although she has difficulty picturing where or when.

'People think you just sit around, plotting the perfect crime. Not me. There's no such thing. It's just how much you can get away with. Wish he'd turn that down.' Randy points to one of the rainbow-hat kids, whose earphones are leaking talk radio. 'Traffic reports always make me sad. Ever since I was a kid.'

Traffic reports remind Marion of her father, of front seats.

'Hold on, honey, too much traffic.' Marion's father is driving her to skating lessons. Marion is holding on.

'Not a great idea, pulling a U-ie in front of the fuzz.' Her father places an open palm protectively on her tummy, which is bulging over the seatbelt, as they swing around. Just like a U, just like he said.

'Whoo! Made it. Don't you ever do that. Do as I say, not as I do. Got it?'

Marion nods, and digs her fingers into the rubbery piece of the door that hugs the bottom of the window. The road ahead is clear. Something unlatches behind her breastbone as they speed up.

One day, when Carl was five, Marion eight and Yvonne ten, their mother reached the end of her rope.

'If you three cannot learn to behave like human beings, I'm reporting us all to the Children's Aid, because, God knows, I could use a little aid right now!'

They went to their rooms. Moments later, Carl was chasing the girls, brandishing a plastic mallet from his mini tool set.

'C'mon,' Yvonne said, and ran downstairs into the dining room, 'we don't want to disturb Ma.' She pulled the tablecloth off the table. 'Under here.'

Under the tented tablecloth was like a secret office where you make important decisions. Yvonne whispered things to Marion, who took notes on her knee.

'Safe,' said Yvonne.

Marion was not convinced. 'Maybe when Dad comes back he'll buy us helmets.'

'He must have just seen our little pea-pod heads sticking up. Bonk! Bonk! Jesus, that hurt,' Yvonne says.

Marion has just arrived at the hospital. Marion and Yvonne are sitting on either side of Carl, who is in a coma. They are waiting for their mother. They are waiting for Carl to wake up.

'I had a goose egg for a week. I guess that was a pretty stupid idea.' Yvonne blinks quickly.

'Well,' says Marion, 'you meant well.'

'Yeah.' Yvonne begins to cry. 'You know, if he comes to, it might not be real. I mean, it might just be the golden hour.'

'What?'

'The golden hour. It's when people who are very sick or gravely injured seem to rally and get better right before the end. It's just a last chance for them to say goodbye, forgive people they've wronged, that kind of thing.'

Forgive people they've wronged? 'Right. Well, how will we know?'

'I guess we won't. We won't know until we know.'

For the first hour Carl is awake, Marion goes to the bathroom five times, stops to check the large wall clock in the hall, following the red second hand, that lucky racehorse. In the bathroom, she washes her hands with the mauve soap from the dispenser, dries them on her skirt.

'What's wrong with you?' says Carl, when she pulls back his bed curtain.

'Too much coffee,' says Yvonne.

And by the time their mother arrives, the golden hour has spun out, as if by wizardry, into a whole golden afternoon.

'Were you drugged, Carl? What were you thinking?'

'It's *on drugs*, Ma, not *drugged*,' Marion corrects.

'So, were you on drugs?'

'The doctors say the marijuana might have helped him, Ma. It's the reason he didn't sustain a lot of injury – his body was so relaxed.' Yvonne flops Carl's hand around to demonstrate.

'Don't social-work me, young lady. We might not be worrying about his body so much if he hadn't got himself hit by a train in the first place. Am I right?' She grabs Carl's hand from Yvonne and presses it to her cheek, which is smeared with tears and travel.

'Chicken or the egg,' says Carl. 'Age-old question.'

'So, this girl. The first time I saw her, I was just paying for my gas – I got this motorbike the guys at the shop let me use – and she looks at me, she looks at me and says, "Wouldn't mind going for a ride on that bike." Yeah, she's one bold piece of work.' Randy stops speaking, reclines his seat, straightens it up, performs a practised two-fingered groom on his moustache. 'Thing is, and this is the thing – I really like this girl. I mean, I could really see myself with her, y'know? I mean, she represents something.'

In the sushi restaurant, Marion had wanted to talk. What she wanted to talk about was availability.

'Yes,' Gene said, 'I'm listening.'

'You are a spectre, Gene. You are a bunch of confused molecules.'

'I thought we agreed that what's most important right now is that I'm committed to you and our projected future.'

Marion thought of the word *projected*. It reminded her of school science films and home movies – catapulted flakes of colour appearing suddenly, inexplicably, on a blank wall. 'You're not listening.'

'I am listening, sweetness, really I am.'

But Marion did not believe that he was. What Sacha did before she began to paint – her palette mixed and at the ready, her mouth slightly open like a slow-motion goldfish – that was listening. Whether Marion herself had ever really listened to Gene was also up for grabs; she was not convinced that waiting your turn – your own tale twisting and turning in your throat – really qualified.

'So, your boyfriend, what's he like?'

'Married.'

'Huh. Married.' Randy leans over her to look out the window. 'Guess we're almost there.'

Another thing Yvonne tells Marion is that she should monitor her self-esteem. Yvonne believes hearts can be charted, fine-tuned. That you can control the shape of your love, squish it into the mould that best suits your mood, so that, at the right moment, it will slide free: solid, quivering and perfectly formed.

'Did you see that? Thought it was a crow, but it was a hawk – you can tell by the way they glide. I got a theory about that, y'know, predators and prey. There was a hawk I used to watch when I was out in the yard, saw it swoop down to catch mice thousands of times.' Randy holds his hands like claws in front of Marion's face. 'We're not so different. And y'know, when things go bad, there's always those people you thought were your buddies, just standin' by, watchin' the carnage. And who can blame them, really? I'd do the same.'

Sometimes Marion tries to imagine it. Sometimes she dreams herself in the engineer's seat: the impact. When she asks Carl, he says nothing, except: 'You know when you taste something and it's so exquisitely disgusting or awesome you know that you will never, ever taste it the same way again? Then sometimes you think you see the taste in places – you see the taste on street signs, in a dog's eyes, or in the patterns in an ashtray. You lick your own skin, because you think you see the taste there. Your molars ache and pine all the fucking time.'

'So, Randy, are you serious about this girl?' Marion feels formal and inappropriately collusive using his name, like a father trying to sound like a peer.

'Oh, I'm serious, all right. I am see-ree-us. But the problem is she's living with her brother and sister-in-law right now, helping out with the kids, saving a bit on rent, y'know? Man, but the way she looks at me, and her arms all solid around my waist on the bike …'

'I've never ridden on a motorcycle before.' This is not true, although it *seems* true as she says it.

'Oh, it's somethin'. Gotta watch out for the black ice in the winter, though, that's for sure.' He taps his fingers on the armrest between them. 'So, Renée, what's the first thing you're gonna do when you get home to Toronto?'

Marion hates these kinds of questions. They are tests designed to ascertain your provenance and domestic aspirations; they make her feel slow in the head. 'I was thinking of painting my apartment,' she says, closing her eyes and pushing herself back into the soft clean paper that hangs over the headrest.

Once, Marion remembers, Sacha had painted something very unlike her normal work. It was relatively realist, and drab – a house that looked to be made out of chocolate perched on a grey cliff overlooking the black churning sea.

'It's called *Yearning*,' she said, tapping the toe of her army boot against the floor tiles. 'Or *House Near Sea*.'

'Who lives there?'

'Me, of course.'

'Right,' said Marion. 'I get you.'

'Yeah, it's not really my style anymore.'

When Marion and Gene first got together, they spent a lot of time in a clinch in his car. He picked her up from work and drove her home in his four-door Volvo and they steamed up the windows making out. Sometimes he showed her pictures of Joyce. In the pictures, Joyce was always in motion, her hair loose and flying free, her mouth frozen mid-exclamation. She had the kind of face that was described in books as having 'planes' and 'mysterious shadows.'

Marion finally convinced Gene that it would be both more practical and more comfortable to grope at each other without the obstacle of the gearshift, but the sex was still frantic and graceless. She was reminded of the slap fights she'd had as a child with Yvonne. Their schoolgirl tussles had been half-hearted – ineffectual flurries of limp-wristed frustration. Neither of them knew how to throw a punch.

The hotel room they rented was dingy and small, and Marion was left with the unenviable task of waking Gene in time for him to get home for supper. This was what made her love Gene, finally: how he slept, his arm slung heavy across her back, face muscles slack and surrendered. He slept as if he were falling through the air, free-form, with no need of a parachute. She imagined that if she had Gene to sleep beside, consistently, at nighttime, his easy slumber might rub off on her. She imagined them entering sleep together.

Sometimes Marion tries to see herself in one of Gene's films, ordering a cappuccino or a Bloody Mary, heading towards the bar or a low oak table. For some reason she is always wearing a pillbox hat in these scenes, and her walk is mincing: half spinster, half strumpet. Then she is sitting with Joyce, who appears relaxed and is not wearing a hat of any kind. They share a plate of onion rings to pass the time.

What does Marion want from Gene, then? Not only distraction and validation, but a more original linkage of happenings, a new means of ordering. Instead, what she is coming to understand is that often a story is just a glint: swift, shiny and vulnerable to vantage point.

'So, my sister, she drives me nuts, always with her Our Saviour this and Our Saviour that ... And I don't really believe in God, y'know, except when it comes to baseball. Last time I was home, I convinced my son to go to a game with me, and we're sitting there in the stands, him all huge and hunched over. Then the pitcher winds up, lets fly, and you can tell, you can just tell that some holy spirit is on the batter's side, 'cause when the bat connects it's like fucking paradise has erupted over that plate, y'know?'

Marion does not know that she will tell Gene Randy's story after all. What she does know is that she could do it; she could love this convict. When she was eleven and her grandfather died, she had forced herself into mini heart attacks. Every night she would wake up, shoulder throbbing, a sensation like somebody opening an umbrella inside her chest. Over-identifying, Yvonne might say. But it was not only empathy, or the power of suggestion – it was more than this. It was an alternate neon reality that flashed inside her, large as advertising. *My accomplice here, among you.*

There is something about the last leg of a journey home that brings to mind the golden hour: anticipation and absolution. The mood on the bus, once raucous with engine noise, impatience, has settled into something almost sweet, more refined than regret. The old man across the aisle from Marion wraps something carefully in tissue paper, pushes it gently into his carry-on, brushes dust from his black dress shoes.

How would Marion forgive the people she's wronged? Have Gene's Joyce to dinner maybe, pardon her for loving and keeping the man she, Marion, cannot surrender? She can envision the candlelight, the courtesies, the napkins shielding their laps, Joyce's animated hair. There is nothing, really, to forgiveness. Maybe even Marion's wayward father could forgive her, forgive her the rage she carries like a large limp bird, draped stubbornly across her body. No, there is nothing to forgiveness; it is finding your way out of the chocolate house on the cliff, into the sting and pound of the surf, into your own battened-down self.

Marion had once tried to explain the golden hour to Carl. 'It's about second chances, reprieves.' She poured him some coffee.

'Sounds more like a lot of waiting, forcing the issue.' He fiddled with Marion's tablecloth. 'Remember when you and Yvonne thought you could hide?'

'Yeah, Mr. Handyman. I kept hoping Dad would come back and put you in your place.'

'No fucking golden hour there, eh?'

'No, but you made a comeback, smartass.'

'I guess I did. You got cream instead of milk?'

At the border, the customs officer ticks a tiny box on a form when Marion reports she has nothing to declare.

Gallons and gallons of water falling over some rocks, a gorge with a terrifyingly turquoise whirlpool, some powdery, blue-haired ladies outside a casino. Beyond that, her city, a city invoked by other nations. And north of that, some trees being felled, some trees being planted. So much shadowy space. Oh, Canada. She is glad to be home.

On the highway into Buffalo, Randy had taken her hand in his. He examined it, then turned it sideways to shake. 'It was nice meeting you, Renée. Good luck with everything.'

'Thanks, you too. It was good talking to you.'

'Yeah, well, that's just my story, I guess … I got this other story I tell myself, about what might actually happen with this girl, if she could get a place of her own, if I could get away from my sister.' He shook his head. 'Man, now there's a good story.'

Marion has a story like this. It is an old story, and borrowed; she once heard her aunt tell it to her mother. Still, she keeps it like a pet, strokes it when she feels at odds. The story goes like this: *Marion's aunt, whose name is Donna, is a young woman, flushed and keen. Donna has a boyfriend who lives in Washington. She has only ever been on three dates with the boyfriend, when they both lived in Australia, where Donna taught for two years. But they've written letters; they are pen pals. Now the boyfriend, whose name is Jonathan, not John, has invited her for a visit. She will take the train from Toronto to Washington. Since it is an occasion, she dresses up. Donna wears a knee-length black skirt, tight, but not too tight, a blouse that is sheer but tasteful and black patent-leather mules. She does not anticipate the arduous limbo of the journey, or, if she does, she does not care. On the platform, other people wait. A man in a beltless trenchcoat bobs his head at her. He is handsome, but short. A girl-toddler rocks back onto her padded bottom, just sits there in the griminess. The girl's mother hums a tune to the railway tracks. Jonathan, who is a lawyer, who is tall, waits for Donna at the other end. When the train finally pulls into the station, it is night, there have been delays. Donna drags her bag to the edge, where a man in a cap hefts it easily into the baggage compartment. The step up is steep; Donna lifts her leg like a karate star, and for a moment her mule dangles dangerously from her foot. Then it falls. Three porters come immediately to her assistance. They have the casual yet weighted stance of officialdom. They assess and confer, then one climbs down onto the tracks, where the rats scurry and duck, busy henchmen in the shadows. Once the chosen porter has located the shoe, he holds it aloft elatedly, like a lover, a lantern clutched in his free hand, illuminating the entire scene.*

MACHAYA

'Stay away from all the big beaches, eh, all the hoo-hah. You don't need that. Just the sand and the sun, that's enough.' Misha's father was sitting at the kitchen table, his empty dinner plate pushed to one side. When he said 'hoo-hah,' he moved his arms suddenly, like a party.

'Léo, are you sure you can't come with us? It's only two weeks – the break, it would do you good.' Misha's mother's voice sounded softer than usual, and as she spoke she poked at a kleenex she had tucked up her sleeve.

'Sophie, you know we've been over this before. This is a crucial time, what with the new shipment coming in. It would be completely stupid for me to leave.'

'Yes, yes.' She ran her fingers through Misha's hair, tugged on his ears, whispered into one of them. 'Alors, ce sera nous deux, seulement, *habibi.*'

'You'll have to take care of your mother, eh, Misha? You're a big boy now. Seven years old. Hold her hand on the airplane.' Misha's father looked at him, waiting. Misha nodded, then watched his father's gaze shift and reconfigure as if there were an interesting TV show playing in the next room.

But Misha had not been altogether sure of the whole idea of a vacation and what it would entail. It seemed to him there were perhaps more pitfalls involved in the process than his father was letting on, more sneaky obstacles to be overcome than were initially obvious to the untrained traveller. He thought he might like to stay home.

Misha's room is at the back of the condo. It is a small room with many windows, so that, in the morning, he wakes to an intense red, his eyelids made transparent by the strength of the sun. At the edge of dream there are sounds: tennis balls donking against the court or thwanging against tautly strung racquets. And this is where he thinks, *Today, vacation*, his red eyes still closed, and the so-very-new sensation of saltwater pulling his skin tight across his bones. He remembers, in the porousness of half-sleep, one hundred watchful shore birds, their legs like oversized french fries, who stood guard around his bed somewhere in the night. He remembers sleep itself: the sensation of being held, gently, by his own body. When he finally, forcefully, opens his eyes, the slow red sun bursts into the white light of southern hospitality. 'Y'all,' says the sun, and really means it. 'Y'all!'

He spends his mornings in the sand, grains stuck like sugar on the backs of his legs, clumping in folds in the crotch of his swim trunks, bits of grit caught with sunshine and saltwater in his scalp.

He meets people on the beach: Jocelyn, a gorgeous, bossy eleven-year-old with sparkly nail polish on her toes, and Evan, a five-and-a-half-year-old whose sun-bleached hair falls in a chunk across his blank blue eyes. Misha hates Evan. He makes him dig the moats of the castles they scoop together, then shoves handfuls of sand back into the shallow trenches while Evan is fetching stones or shells from the edge of the ocean. He hates Evan because Evan lets him give the orders and sabotage the results, hates him for the floppiness of his manner and his slow, unblinking trust.

'I saw what you did to Evan. You're nothing but a piece of dirt under my feet.' Jocelyn crosses her arms over her chubby torso, her puffy new boobs caught in the crooks of her elbows. 'I'm gonna tell my mom, and she's gonna tell your mom, and then you're gonna see what you're gonna see.'

Jocelyn has a way of stretching out her threats, elaborating on what would otherwise be more effective retorts. For Misha, this makes her both more attractive and slightly less intimidating. It means he has time to think while she is talking. He knows she will only turn him in if there is nothing better to do. Above, the sun is a clean bright ball high in the endless sky. The ocean laps at Jocelyn's perfect pink toes. She stares at him, then grabs her beach bag and stomps off.

Misha's mother is wading out into the ocean, on her tiptoes, her palms poised above the glitzy waves. Misha is watching her, and she knows it. She looks back at him, at the toys strewn pell-mell across the beach blanket.

'*Machaya!*' she shouts out. 'What a life!'

Misha says the word to himself, *machaya*, and pulls a smooth green piece of glass from the sand. He holds it up to the sun, peers through it and scopes the length of the beach. He can see Jocelyn and her mother making their way down from the motel. Jocelyn is half-running, her feet crazy and uncertain in her flip-flops.

He doesn't feel like dealing with her, plodding through whatever elaborate punishment she may have concocted. He is weary of this whole vacation with its constant state of sand and sun. *Six more days*. He misses the quietness of his playroom, the grit and dash of the schoolyard, snow.

Misha's mother, now waist-deep, is already moving her arms in heart-shaped formations in the water in front of her. Jocelyn has spotted Misha and is flip-flopping purposefully in his direction. He turns away from her pushy girl's body, squints through the glass at his mother, who is still fake-swimming. Then she trips, he thinks, is caught for a second in an underwater crumple. Then, screaming. Like he has never heard before and at first does not believe, until he sees other people running towards the sound that has so abruptly pierced the morning.

Later, after the intermittent light of the ambulance has retreated into the stew of pink balconies, magnolia blossoms and asphalt that coats the city, and Jocelyn's mother has taken charge of him, Misha closes his eyes against the worry tattooed across her face.

'I'm going to call your dad, okay, Misha? Okay?'

Misha stares at her, with her orange and yellow sarong, so strangely tied, so that the ends stick out like tiny extra hands from her hip.

'It's the shock,' she whispers knowingly to Jocelyn, and leads her away by the elbow. Jocelyn peers back at him over her shoulder. *Shock*, her eyes say, *it's the shock*.

But Misha does not feel shock, a sensation he associates with suddenness and electricity. Instead what he feels is a slowness like swimming, and an unwillingness to become excited by the events of the day, which, it seems to him, have been unfolding at a safe, shimmery distance. Jocelyn's mother has draped a blanket across his shoulders, and plumped the pillows on the sofa bed to make him more comfortable. He is not tired, and he can hear rustlings and murmurs from the kitchen, a steady lowing of anxiety. He shifts the pillows around to create a small fort for his head, buries his nose in the cracks between the cushions.

Misha understands that, somehow, he is guilty of something. A lack of vigilance, or a misunderstanding grown fat with its own mistaken importance. He has allowed himself to fall, artlessly, into this vacation and its trappings, and, in some small, whispered way, is responsible for the terrible way it has evolved.

When the plane first touched down in Florida, Misha had watched as people clapped and turned to each other with congratulatory smiles and brisk, happy nods. The stewardesses fussed dutifully and warned the passengers not to unbuckle their seat belts until the *bong* had sounded. But Misha saw that his mother unbuckled anyway, sighed and filled her abdomen with air as if it were the seat belt itself and not their airborne state that had kept her movements restricted, stilted. He reached out his hand to hold her back, then changed his mind and turned to the woman next to him, who shifted from side to side, pulled a makeup bag from her carry-on and fished out a tubular case with tiny snaps on the front. Inside was a lipstick in the sleek shape of a bullet and a small rectangular mirror fastened onto the case's flapping lid. The woman, whose name was Christa, unscrewed the lipstick lid and swivelled the stick of colour up into the stale atmosphere of the cabin. She brought the case up to her face, angled it, then pressed the lipstick along her bottom lip. Then she turned to Misha, held the tiny mirror up to his face and passed him the tube.

'Here, you try,' she said, and smiled, her darkened lips stretching to either side of her tiny turned-up nose.

'Okay,' he said, taking the lipstick and tilting his head to see in the mirror. His mother was also sifting through her bag, stacking passports, pens and brochures in her lap.

He finished putting on the lipstick and puckered his lips at Christa, sucking in his cheeks as he had seen his mother do. Christa laughed and puckered too.

'That's it, sweetie. Perfect.' She reached across the seat and cupped his chin in her hand. 'You look perfect.'

Earlier in the trip there had been a meal in small, square plastic sections – chicken and round tasteless potatoes, then sweet icinged cake for dessert. At the end of the long narrow aisle next to Christa was a metal bathroom with a swift sucking toilet and a kleenex box stuck to the wall. Misha had visited the bathroom twice, by himself, following the curved sides of the plane that surrounded him like a shining city night, its long line of peepholes blinking out into the blue, seemingly solid air. He had watched his mother slide one of the peephole's sliding panels up like an eyelid, had leaned over her to look out and down. Below the plane, on the ground, unadulterated blobs of turquoise and hunter green nudged up against each other. Above the blobs, everywhere, always, were the odd top sides of clouds, stretched, puddled or piled under the plane's sharp silver wings. And through it all, his mother, with her voice like an animal that lived inside him, nuzzling and fierce. On the ground, behind him, in a newly snow-whitened city called Montreal, was his father, with his smooth blue suit and quick hard hugs.

'You'll be all right alone?' he had asked, but it was, Misha thought, less like a question than an announcement, his mouth shaping the words that would carry them through to the other side, the other country. 'Remember, you'll take the St. Petersburg shuttle – it leaves every half-hour,' he said, his eyes skimming over the other passengers boarding. 'Looks like you've got a lot of peppers on your flight.'

'Léonard, ne sois pas raciste.' Misha's mother leaned into his father, placed her hand on the lapel of the blue suit.

'I'm not being racist, I'm being realistic. They're a buncha meshugenahs, always with the smoking and the drinking and the junk food ... ' He looked down at Misha, winked at him. Misha winked back with both eyes, feeling stupid and pleased, which was how he always felt with his father.

'Viens, mon chérie.' His mother pulled her purse up on her shoulder, then took Misha's hand and reached up to kiss her husband.

Then it had all been like a big show: the handing over of things – tickets, small pillows decorated with tiny maple leaves, scratchy blankets, empty trays and bulging brown wastepaper bags – the view from the peepholes, Christa the friendly seatmate and the smiling-strict stewardesses, with their questions and pats and pinches. And now, finally, the applause, and the deep pilot voice wishing them a pleasant stay and informing them, convincingly, of the time and the weather.

'There's a dead snake on the beach. I'm going to operate on it.' Misha flung out his arm in front of him, half point, half showmanship. 'You can come if you like.'

Jocelyn hurled a dismembered crab claw at him but agreed. Evan, who was busy scrabbling in the sandcastle's shallow moat, followed them.

The snake was not actually a snake; it was a trailing stem of seaweed that had washed ashore, but once the fiction had been established, neither Misha nor Jocelyn felt any need to dismantle it.

'Water snakes are the most deadly of all snakes,' Jocelyn pronounced, holding her arms out in a prohibitive, parent-like gesture. 'First we must ensure the area is clear of any dangerous particles.' She marched around the periphery of the snake site, inspecting the sand, reaching down every so often to nudge at something with her finger. Misha and Evan stood at a respectful distance, eyeing the snake with reverence and caution.

Finally, Jocelyn declared the area safe, and the boys moved in to begin the job. The snake's skin sliced open easily with the edge of a seashell, although its innards were not as satisfyingly gunky as they had hoped. Misha sent Evan to fetch a bucket and spade to aid in the dissection, and reabsorbed himself in the work.

When Jocelyn was concentrating she sometimes sang a little, under her breath, tuneless.

'What is that song?' Misha asked, after they had been hacking at the snake for what felt like a long time. Jocelyn didn't hear him at first, continued picking and peeling at the snake's skin with her stubby fingernails. He leaned over her, spoke into her face like a microphone. 'Jo-ce-lyn. What is that song?'

And her eyes changed somehow, the quiet fixedness required by the task at hand replaced by something momentarily wild and zinging. She stood up, cleared her throat.

'It's James Brown. It's my dad's favourite song.' She closed her eyes and tapped her open hand against her hip.

Her eyes snapped open and skidded over Misha and Evan to the cheering throngs she had conjured on the beach. She paused for a beat to hiss at Misha. 'It's called "I Feel Good."'

A couple of teenagers wading in the water stopped for a moment, then turned and snickered, lording their beautiful hybrid bodies over the show. Jocelyn, undeterred, increased the volume, stomped forward semi-sexily, then threw back her head, opened her mouth to the Florida sky.

The teenagers were now laughing raucously, adding their caws to the cranky din of the seagulls. Jocelyn stopped singing, and it was like a power outage or an eclipse. Misha inched his way over on the sand, reached up to touch her elbow. She flicked his hand away angrily, shoved his shoulder out of her performance space, then turned, trembling, towards the shore.

'Fuck. You.' She was crying, shaking her fist at the teenaged boy and girl, who had already begun kicking their way through the surf, untouchable.

The girl smiled apologetically at Jocelyn, then, with a delicate laxity, spoke. 'This machine's out of order, fuck yourself and save a quarter.' She shrugged, orbited gracefully away from Jocelyn, the two staring boys and the stringy seaweed.

All of this made Misha tired. How many years before he could stand and sing, like Jocelyn, two young disciples snared in his glamorous wake? And how long after that before he could kick his way through the sand, his supremacy glaringly casual and far-flung?

Evan had returned dutifully to the problem of the snake. Jocelyn crouched to poke at a silvery strand, sniffed, then stood up again. 'I'm bored. I'm gonna see if the ice cream guy's here.'

Misha didn't want to leave but knew that without Jocelyn the game would devolve into a sham. This was the alchemy of play; a game could spring, like a god or a genie, from the ether, and dissolve just as quickly, leaving nothing but curious babblers and wrong-headed believers in its golden wake.

Evan was already scrambling after Jocelyn. Misha sat still and stubborn for a moment before following.

On the sixth night of the vacation, Misha woke before dawn, having dreamt of his father. He stumbled to the window, checked the tennis court and the pool for a sign. In the dream, his father was laughing, his head cocked to one side under the half-hearted spray of the poolside shower.

'Met any little friends?' he called out to Misha, then spat a smooth two-pronged plume of water between his teeth. The water landed with a splash on Misha's shoulder and ran, tickling, down his chest. Misha stared at his father, who grinned, then shook his head briskly, sending more tiny bits of water flying through the air. 'Bon voyage, eh, Misha, bon voyage!' he called, then stepped from the shower, dry and dressed, his blue suit aglow in the sunlight.

After breakfast, it began to rain, the drops tippling down from the undersides of large taffy-coloured clouds. Misha wandered the apartment, which had a clean, boxy feel to it, so unlike his apartment at home with its creaking wooden floors and sloping walls. The low ceilings and sharp angles made him feel large and businesslike. He stepped outside to patrol the hallway, which was also a long strip of balcony that girded the outside of the building. The wind was strong, and, for a moment, Misha was scared at the way it whipped through the large American flag in the parking lot. The sound made him think of wrestling and choking.

Through the window next to the apartment door he could see a TV glowing like a friendly beacon. Misha knew TV, he liked TV. He leaned in close to the window and cupped his hands around his face to cut down on the glare. The show was a funny one; he could tell by the way the people moved, as if they had important places to go but not really. Misha watched until he saw a man inside the apartment coming towards him with a cereal bowl. Then he ducked and ran back inside for his own breakfast.

'No beach today, 'tit chou,' said Misha's mother, and poured herself another cup of coffee. 'No beach today.'

No beach, but after Misha had finished his toast, Jocelyn's mom called to invite them to the outlet mall, a glorious cluster of shops with stuff for cheap. They took the rental car, a white Ford with a whirring air conditioner and a smell like lemons and dirty pennies. On the bridge into the city, the sky began to clear, sending a rainbow arcing down through the yellow-grey smog that hung over the buildings. Jocelyn pointed out the window to a salmon-coloured condominium complex with two matching kidney-shaped pools.

'Someday,' she whispered loudly, 'this will all be mine.' Then she poked Misha in the ribs and drew her mouth into a lipsticked pout. Misha crossed his eyes and stuck out his bottom lip until she laughed.

'Here, try this,' Jocelyn said, drawing Misha's head towards her, so that their foreheads touched. 'Stare into my eyes.'

'No,' said Misha. 'Gross.'

'You are such a baby.' She took his head again. 'Now, just stare into my eyes as hard as you can.'

Misha stared. Jocelyn's eyes were a flat brown, the irises ringed with bands of tiny green stars. As he stared, her eyes floated together, connected themselves above her nose. He blinked. Behind Jocelyn's linked eyes, out the car window, the world went rushing past, street signs and palm trees and cars just like theirs, going shopping.

'Ha! You see?' she shouted. 'We're cyclops!' She shoved him away triumphantly.

'What's a cyclop?' Misha asked, and felt immediately ill-equipped.

'It's a monster? With one eye? I can't believe you've never heard about it before. It's like the song.' She looked at him, waiting.

He shook his head and looked out the window.

'My one-eyed only love!' Jocelyn belted it out.

'Quiet in the back, you two,' her mother called, but in a nice way.

Jocelyn swore under her breath and turned her back on Misha.

At the mall, the mothers insisted on entering every beckoning store, where they fingered fabrics and flipped over price tags to compare. Misha's mother tried on a pair of half-price cross-trainers at the discount store but they were too small, no luck. Misha lingered over a pair of black and white wingtips. Magic shoes. Or at least the type of shoes a magician might wear. Jocelyn tried on a pair of platform sandals with daisies glued onto the toe strap.

'You look like a hussy,' said her mother, and pulled the shoes from her feet.

In a jungly beach-wear store, both the mothers donned sarongs, then stood like overstuffed tropical birds, eyes squinting in appraisal, in front of the long mirrors.

'You're so slim,' said Misha's mother admiringly, patting down her thighs.

'Well, you know, you don't get fat drinkin' Diet Coke and sleepin' alone.' Jocelyn's mother patted at her own thighs and sucked in her cheeks. Misha watched his mother watching Jocelyn's mother, her eyes widening and narrowing in a shuttering of understanding. There were lessons to be learned at the outlet mall.

In the food court you could get fast food from any part of the world. Misha chose China because of the triangular hats the happy men in the picture were wearing. Jocelyn chose California because of the waitress's deep tan and unerring smile, and the mothers ordered sandwiches and salads from the deli, which was just plain American food. They found a booth near the centre of the court, and Jocelyn slid her bum in next to Misha's.

'Mom, after this can we go to the drugstore? 'Cause I really wanna try that new hair stuff to lighten my bangs. So can we?' Jocelyn reached over Misha to tug on her mother's sleeve.

'Honey, Sophie and I just want a bit of peace and quiet to chat. Why don't you and Misha go get some ice cream?' The mothers pulled money out of their wallets, and Jocelyn glared at Misha, but grabbed his hand and pulled him away.

Their first night in Florida, Misha and his mother had gone for dinner, just the two of them, like a secret club. They chose a fish place near the beach which was also a bar, but you could get pop if you didn't drink beer. The waitress's name was Luanne and she smelled like something close to the earth and bursting. Misha's mother wasn't very hungry, so Luanne let her have the kid's portion, and she refilled Misha's pop glass for free. The grouper sandwich was delicious, the white bun giving way to the crunchiness of the batter between his teeth, and his mother looked so beautiful, with her hair pulled off her face and her green baseball T-shirt. He wished his father could see them, and this wishing, this picturing, made Misha glad – his mother, himself and Luanne, all bent over the menu, deciding, and his father watching them from an unimaginable distance.

At the ice cream counter, Jocelyn ordered bubble-gum flavour and flirted with the scooper, a fourteen-year-old boy with an earring in his lip. Misha counted his change and came up short.

'God, you practically have to know another language to order coffee these days,' Jocelyn's mother was saying, pointing to her café au lait as Misha approached the table. 'Where I come from we call that milky coffee.'

Misha's mother looked down, sipped twice at her milky coffee. 'How long have you been separated from your husband?'

'Oh, we haven't seen hide nor tail of him since Jocelyn was two. Doesn't even pay his support. Had to hire a lawyer again this year to go after him. He just dumped his latest girlfriend, now she's after him too. Apparently, he owes her money. And it's not that he doesn't make enough, you know – he's a salesman, and a good one. He's just a goddamn weasel is all, excuse my French.' Jocelyn's mother took a bite of her danish. 'What about you, Sophie, what does your husband do?'

'Oh, he owns a furniture store. Quite successful, but still just starting out, you understand.' Misha's mother sat up in her chair and adjusted the sunglasses she had perched on her head.

'Sure, I know how it is.'

Misha crept up behind his mother and placed his hands over one of her eyes. *Maman is a cyclops*, he thought, and cleared his throat. 'Maman. Mom. I need a dollar.'

Misha's mother dug in her purse without looking at him, then passed him a handful of coins, coins that seemed less shiny but somehow more substantial, with their bunch of serious presidents, than the ones from home: the loon, the leaf, the beaver, the caribou – all of them backing the snooty queen. He jingled the coins in his palm, counted them.

Two months ago Misha and his father had driven to a small sports shop in Côte-Saint-Luc where Misha's father knew the owner, Art. Misha wanted to spend his Hanukkah gelt on a new pair of skates. Art was up front when they arrived, stacking shin pads next to the counter.

'Hey, Leo, long time no see. This your son?' He pointed to Misha, a shin pad hanging from his arm like an armadillo.

Misha nodded.

'Yes, this is Misha.' He nudged Misha forward. 'We're looking for some hockey skates. And you, how's the family?'

Art pulled the last shin pad from the box and placed it on the top of the pile. 'Oi-a-baruch! Marcia's all right now, but you should have seen her last week – she had the flu like you wouldn't believe.'

Misha looked around the store. He could see the skates he wanted hanging on the wall next to a poster of Wayne Gretzky. He tugged on his father's sleeve.

'You want my money now, I suppose,' his father said, reaching for his wallet. 'There, now it's your money.' He tucked some bills into Misha's back pocket and pushed him in the direction of the skates.

When Art had fetched the right size from the stockroom, Misha's father came over and kneeled in front of Misha to help him. He pulled the large, stiff tongue back from the body of the skate while Misha pushed hard with his foot. What Misha remembered most was the ridge at the back of the skate, the way it felt scraping against the back of his heel as his toes slid satisfyingly into place.

His father was still kneeling, his head bent so that Misha could see the hair growing above his collar on the back of his neck. He had watched his mother cut those hairs with long silver scissors, the tips of her fingers poking through the grips as she instructed his father, softly, to turn this way, move that way.

'Can I have these?' Misha nodded his head at the skates, which his father was now lacing with small insistent tugs.

'You've got to get them really tight,' his father said, straightening up. He reached down and squeezed Misha's shoulder, then looked over at Art, who was busy behind the counter. 'It's your money,' he added, and dusted off his pants with his open hands.

'Why didn't your husband come, then, Sophie? He must be able to afford it, with the store and all. Would be nice to have a man around.' She made a big clown wink at Misha's mother and patted Misha on the back.

'Oh, yes,' said Misha's mother, laughing high and quick, 'he's just very busy with his work. Very busy, you know how it is ...' She sipped at her café au lait again.

How it is? Misha thought. *How is it?*

'Sure, I know, they're always busy with something, aren't they?' Jocelyn's mother laughed a laugh that wasn't really a laugh and wiped at the corner of her red mouth.

The night before they had left for Florida, after Misha had gone to bed, he heard his mother and his father in the next room, arguing. He pushed aside his covers, walked quietly to his door and opened it, careful not to hit the doorstop coil and send it thrumming back and forth. Then he crouched against the baseboards and listened.

'Sophie, you're being so unreasonable. There is no big trick to this decision. The store needs me, that's all there is to it.' Misha's father sighed, then made a final snuffling sound.

'This is not the sum of life – a dilemma and then a decision, a dilemma and then a decision! Why do you always think we are in control? Don't you think Misha might want you there?' Her voice reminded Misha of a crow, the way its black wings beat for an instant against the air before it took flight. 'You waste nothing, and these decisions you make – they mean everything. Ce n'est pas comme ça qu'on vit sa vie. Dilemma, decision, dilemma, decision … ' She began to cry.

Misha stood up then and brought his foot down heavily on the doorstop, so that the sound of the thick coil vibrating followed him back to his bed.

The condo was not far from the beach, but in the afternoons, when it was hottest, Misha's mother liked to sit by the pool, where there was more shade and the water was clear and diluted. She asked him to sit on a deck chair while she took a shower.

'I'll be right back, okay, Mish?' She pulled a towel from her shoulder bag and spread it across the sticky white weave of the chair. Misha nodded. There was a beefy man with a white crewcut bobbing up and down in the pool. Misha liked his look, so unlike his father or his grandfather, both small and wiry. He stared at the man.

'What's your name, son?' The man had pulled himself over to the edge of the pool and allowed his legs to float up behind him like drowned sausages.

'Misha.'

'Mee-cha? Well, I'm pleased to meetcha too.' The man's laugh was a rumble that caught and broke, then caught again, somewhere between his throat and his stomach.

Misha's mother had stopped. 'Michael is his name,' she said. 'Mike. It's his first time here.'

'Well, Mike,' said the man, 'are you enjoying your stay?'

'Sure am,' said Misha, which was something he had heard Jocelyn say to her mother when she asked if she was hungry or thirsty. His own mother looked at him, surprised, but she seemed pleased, and waved at him on her way to the showers.

There was another man at the pool's gate. This one was tall and bald, and he was with a fat woman who limped a little. They sat on the edge of the pool with their feet in the water.

'Another hot one, eh, Walt?' The first man was speaking to the second man.

'Sure is. Got the air conditioning cranked right up.' The tall man splashed some water on his chest, then rubbed it into his arms. The woman was lowering herself into the pool, her mouth already forming bubbles. Misha watched her as she swam. She was breaststroking around the edge, her lips barely grazing the bright translucence of the surface.

'How many you gonna do today, Margie?' It was the beefy man again.

'Oh, I guess I'll just keep going till I'm tired out.' Margie splashed him a little as she passed. Misha liked these people, their big bodies and the way their words seemed to expand as they spoke them.

'Went into town yesterday for the breakfast special. Shoulda got there a bit earlier, though – almost all the French toast was gone. Isn't that right, Margie?' Walt turned to Margie, who nodded into her chest and swallowed water, then coughed and swam to the side. 'What about you, Rick, you make it in for the Early Bird?'

'Yeah, we were there real early. Stopped by the mall for a while afterwards. May wanted to check out the beach-wear sale. It's such a pain in the butt these days – so many of the shops been bought up by the Chinks. Soon as you turn your back they're chattering away – hi-yah this and hon-yah that.' Rick was making frightening rabbit faces as he spoke, biting down hard on his lower lip. Misha watched as he hoisted his elbows up onto the pool deck. There was a bikinied woman tattooed on his bulky shoulder.

Margie was nodding quickly at him. 'It's the same thing in Philly. You go into a shop and as soon as you've got your back turned it's Jewish this and Jewish that.'

At school, back in Montreal, there was a boy called Dickweed, even though, Misha had divined, this was not his true name. There were times, he knew, when it was all right to call the boy, who was lumbering and petty, by this name, but there were other times – for instance, when his mother led him by the hand from the back doors – when it was wise to remain silent. And it was the same with French. His mother spoke French, and Misha spoke French, and many people in Montreal spoke French, but at school, speaking French, being French, was a little like being Dickweed, only worse, since it could cling to you like something that stuck on your shoe and would not shake free, even outside the boundaries of the play-ground. And now, Misha understood, in this hot place, next to this rectangle of a pool, it was unwise to speak Yiddish, that half-imaginary language of prayer and exclamation. It was complicated but also simple, how he had to behave, the words he spoke – words backed by thoughts so ineffable they were less thoughts than the elongated shadows of an impulse, the grey aftermath of intention.

Misha's mother had returned from the shower and was sitting, dripping, on the chair next to him. 'On va nager bientôt, okay?' she murmured, and opened her book. Misha took his mini cars from his mother's bag and went to sit closer to Walt and Rick, who were lounging in the shade of a palm tree.

'Where exactly did they say they're from?' Walt asked.

'Montreal, Canada. You know, part of that country north of Buffalo,' Rick said, laughing. 'But it sounds like she's got a Spanish accent or something so I'm not so sure.'

It was true. Misha was from Montreal, and so was his mother, but before that she was from France, and before that, Egypt. His father had been born, like him, in Montreal, but Misha's great-grandfather was from Russia, a land older and colder than Canada. There were reasons his mother had moved the way she did, hopping borders, straddling languages. Misha knew the word: *apatride*. Without country. But in his mind the stories had melded, coalesced into something confusing or compelling, depending on the day, or the hour, so that the Egyptian sun beat down, relentless, on the bare head of a French schoolgirl, and an old man wearing a fur coat and a salt-and-pepper beard galloped by on a shaggy camel towards a snow-capped pyramid. In the midst of these fantasies, Misha sometimes found himself caught in a web of anxiety not unlike the feeling he got when he heard certain fairy tales read aloud. He could sense that the family stories, too, were hiding something – a wolf, or a witch with a grudge. There were two things he knew for certain: there was always something to be afraid of, whether it be in the woods or the desert, and everyone, everywhere, came from somewhere else.

'Michael! Michael!' someone was calling. Someone he knew. He looked up from his cars. It was his mother. This mother he knew like he knew his own instinctive, fleeting thoughts.

'Michael, I think you've had enough of the sun – your shoulders are starting to burn.' She began gathering up his toys, then stopped and pulled him close. '*Habibi*,' she whispered.

And now his mother is in the hospital, felled by some underwater thing.

Misha hears the phone ring and thinks of his father, far away and perhaps working. Or thinking, his hand swiping at his black hair. Sometimes, after school, his mother drops him off at Granowsky's, Your Furniture Store, to stay with his father while she does her errands. Misha sits in a chair in the small office at the back of the store and listens to his father speak, slow and careful – as if he were trying to convince someone to come in from the laneway for supper – on the sleek white phone. Sometimes Misha wanders the showroom, steps quietly into wardrobes and stays there inhaling the black forest scent until he hears his father locking up.

The ring is loud and repeats, jangling and hurtling through space. He clenches his teeth, wills it to stop. Instead, from across the kilometres, he thinks he can see his father look up from whatever it is he is so intent on doing and peer at him across the border that separates them. Peering and scowling, as if Misha himself has caused the phone to ring on both ends, to interrupt. And maybe Misha has. It is possible he has chosen incorrectly: the wrong word or gesture, a botched thought.

Behind his father, Misha thinks he can make out his mother's navy winter coat, bulky and worn, still draped over the banister where she left it. He wants to touch it, but it has become one of the signs and signals for home he now strains to remember, along with the clanging sound of his hockey stick against the metal staircase to his front door and the signature his breath used to make on the cold air.

'The hospital called. Your mother is fine, honey, just fine. She'll be able to come home tomorrow.' Jocelyn's mom is bouncing on her toes excitedly, again plumping the pillows beside Misha's head.

He reaches down into his pocket, feels for the piece of green glass that is still there, smooth and waiting. Then, because it seems she expects him to do or say something, he pulls it out, holds it up to the light and winks at her with both eyes.

Jocelyn has found a book on stingrays in the local library, which she brings to the beach two days later, a day before Misha and his mother are scheduled to return home. Evan has already left, embarrassing both Misha and Jocelyn with drooly, teary hugs. Misha's mother is fine behind her novel, the bandage around her instep glowing against her sun-darkened skin. Jocelyn reads to Misha in a radio announcer's voice, punctuating each phrase with a grave downturn in voice.

'"The stab from a stingray not only injects poison but also cuts and tears the flesh, and many people who have trodden on a stingray lying in shallow water have had to have stitches in their feet. The effect of the poison is immediate and inflammation spreads around the wound almost as soon as the spine has penetrated."'

She shows Misha a picture of the stingray, photographed from above, undulating and huge in the water. The creature hovers, just below the surface, unfurling in the underwater breeze like the flag of some misty, undiscovered country. It looks soft and flowing, incapable of instigating the heart-stalling shrieks his mother emitted. It occurs to him she may have been faking it. He glares at her, happy and safe and reclining on her brightly patterned beach towel.

'Hey, Joss, you wanna go for a walk?' He feels tough today, invincible. Jocelyn considers him a moment, registers the combative stance, the shrewd challenge in his eye.

'Sure.' She brushes some sand daintily from the backs of her thighs. 'Where to?'

'Thataway.' He points towards the pier and sets off, lifting his knees slightly higher than usual as he walks. Jocelyn trails behind, holding her sun hat on her head like a southern belle.

'We could pretend we're in the desert dying of thirst, and our camel just collapsed,' says Misha, thinking hero, thinking rescue.

'Nah,' says Jocelyn, and that is that.

Misha can tell by the sun that it is nearing noon; soon the mothers will be tapping at their watches, mouthing *lunchtime* as they sort through their beach bags. He presses onwards, but Jocelyn is so slow, with her ugly hat. Up ahead he can see a small crowd on the beach, their heads drooped down, wondering at something washed up. Behind him Jocelyn has stumbled on an oasis, is draped across a piece of driftwood with an abandoned teen magazine.

Misha pauses for a moment, digs his heels into the wet sand. The problem with Jocelyn is that even when she's ignoring you, she's somehow not. She nags and pulls at your plans until they unravel to the point of insubstantiality.

But Misha is now nearing the attraction on the beach, and Jocelyn shows no sign of following. He counts seven grey-haired onlookers, then skirts the periphery of the group, stations himself at the edges, too far to see the centre, but close enough to hear a man's gruff, proprietary voice.

'I tell ya, they're just like the trout I used to fish up in Lake Michigan – they put up a good fight when you hook 'em, and a bigger fight when you get 'em to shore.'

Misha pushes his way closer to the man, fighting his way through the veiny calves of the assembled retirees. Finally, he finds himself on the inside of the ragged circle, and, crouched unobtrusively, takes in the sight of the fisherman's catch.

It is a stingray. Smaller and meatier-looking than the one in the book, but a stingray nonetheless. And still alive, its rubbery wings flapping and slapping noisily against the edge of the ocean.

Misha closes his eyes and allows some facts to tumble around inside him: His mother is fine. His father is in Montreal. You should stay away from the hoo-hah at the beach. There are fathers who leave. They take their bags of things and their money with presidents or snooty queens, and they leave. Water snakes are the most deadly of all snakes. The whole of the French language is actually a swear word. Shock is a made-up thing, made up by Jocelyn and her weirdo mother.

He inches around so that he can examine the stingray's tail, a long ropy extension that runs down the centre of the body. He wants to grab on to it, to heft the stingray above his head, swing it round and round like a lasso. Once, on another beach, Misha's father filled his small red plastic sand bucket to the rim with lakewater, then swung the bucket up and over. Upside down! And the water did not spill.

'It's gravity!' his father called out, to Misha's round eyes, wide above his open mouth. 'It controls the oceans. It's what keeps us from hurtling off the earth!' Then he set the bucket down, where it sat, rocking slightly, the water dribbling over the edges.

Misha reaches out towards the stingray.

'You touch that you'll be sick for a good twenny-four hours, if not longer.' The fisherman is standing above him, his sneaker planted between Misha's outstretched hand and the ridged tail. Someone in the crowd is curious.

'What are you going to do with it?' It is a petite, well-packaged woman, her pastel pink T-shirt tucked and poofed lovingly into the waistband of her khaki shorts.

'Them's good eatin'. You just take some cookie cutters to the wings, I tell ya, they taste just like scallops.' The fisherman grins at the woman, who backs up a little.

Misha withdraws his hand, but the impulse is still there, surging inside him like an ancient mission.

In the sky overhead, a jet plane spews a fluffy white trail. Misha would like to be on that plane.

Soon it will be everything in reverse: the drive to the airport, the airplane itself, the weather, so uniform and unflappable above the clouds, suddenly transformed into something brittle and unforgiving on the ground.

Once arrived, and seated for dinner, Misha's father will examine him, then hold tightly to the edge of the dining room table, as if trying to make a point, only instead he will ask a question.

'So, son, how was it?'

And Misha will long for it: the scent of suntan lotion buzzing like an amiable insect inside his sinus cavities, the big-busted friendliness of a Florida waitress ricocheting around inside his small heart and the temporary relief from a life that seems, suddenly, to be accumulating around and inside him without his sanction.

He will try to tell the vacation like a story, but what comes rushing forth will instead be an excited verbal miscellany, punctuated by too many *and then*s and marred by a breathlessness he cannot control.

'Mee-sha! Oh, Mee-sha!' It is Jocelyn.

Misha takes one last look at the stingray, whose wings seem to tire for a moment before they burst into strange, violent flight, sending the body up and over, so that the tail rests in the grip of a wave.

'Mee-sha!' Jocelyn is getting closer, jerking her head this way and that, searching. Misha jumps out from the crowd, ambushes the helpless damsel with his stealthy adventurer ways.

'Yeah. As if.' Jocelyn jumps up and down in an effort to see past the people.

'It's just a bunch of seaweed, stupid,' says Misha. There will be no sharing of the stingray.

'Zero times zero is how much I care,' says Jocelyn, and skips ahead, then turns around and sticks out her tongue. 'Race ya, big man!' Sprinting, hat in hand, all the way to the mothers. All the way home.

CONGRATULATIONS, REALLY

The raid is Katie's idea. Afterwards, and in years to come, she will try to convince herself that Tatyana had somehow wiled her into it without saying a word. Katie knows that this would not have been beyond Tatyana's abilities, but she also knows it is only a slim slice of a larger, more ragged truth.

'We'll put some masks on, and just, I dunno, do some tattoos on their faces. Or toothpaste. Toothpaste might be good.' Katie rifles through her makeup bag.

'We should just spy on the counsellors.' Tatyana is reclining on Katie's bunk, painting her nails. 'I think it's raining.'

It is raining, a soft, barely there rain that shushes against the roof of the cabin.

'It's just drizzle. C'mon, it's Saturday night.' Katie pulls the leg of some long johns she has scissored into a disguise over her head, and swings the door wide to show the way. The prospect of being out in the wild of the nighttime woods has opened another secret door inside her; she is impatient, and eager to impress Tatyana with her boldness.

At the fork of the trail, Tatyana stops and points to the crook of a pine tree. 'Shhh, porcupine.' They pause for a moment to observe the bristling dark form. 'They're really shy.'

It is not difficult to get into the boys' cabin; no one locks their doors at camp, and the counsellors have left to smoke cigarettes and play cards in the lodge. Still, the girls take their time, place more secret agent–type emphasis on their actions than is perhaps necessary. Once inside, however, they are unnerved by the normalcy of the scene. The cabin is set up exactly like their own, the bunk beds leaning against the walls, towels and sweatshirts dangling from the rafters. There are no tiny tools of beauty scattered here – eyelash curlers, lipsticks, mascara wands – but the same all-purpose flashlights and compasses line the window sills. The smell is different, though – it is the smell of clean boys' sweat, beery, without the edge of alcohol. But it is not until they look closely at the sleeping shapes on the beds that something snags inside them. It is a snag and then a surge. A surge of what? Power, yes, at looking down on these small-seeming boys, taken from their taunts and tumbles, laid low by sleep. But, also: a muffled astonishment at the unchecked rustlings and cuddlings of creatures far from their mothers.

'You start at that end, we'll meet in the middle.' Tatyana uncaps a black magic marker and walks towards the bunk closest to the door.

Their efforts are unexceptional at first – double lines on the cheeks to denote Indian war paint, a mound of toothpaste next to the pillow – but, with a few tries, and the boys' continued lack of awareness, they sabotage less gingerly.

'Check this out,' Katie hisses. She has ringed her target's mattress with toothpaste and squiggled sperm-like mounds on his chin and forehead.

'Almost done,' says Tatyana. 'You take the last one.'

There is something different about the last one. At first, Katie thinks he must be awake, and is snared for a second in his accusatory stare. But then she realizes that although his eyes are open, he is not seeing her. He's dead. She feels a not-unpleasant roiling in the space just below her ribcage. His eyes are so round and bright, afloat in his dark face like twin suns misplaced in the night. She crouches down next to him and lays her hand on his forehead.

'Tatyana,' Katie says.

Tatyana does not turn to look until the boy sits up, sleeping bag bunched, the sudden stink of urine wafting from his lap, his eyes still fixed on some inflexible future.

There will be other points in Katie's life where her hand will rise, unbidden, to her mouth, as if to contain something: a shriek, a sharp refusal, a sigh or a wholly inappropriate guffaw. No matter. Hand to mouth, automatic and universal. This is the first.

Katie's mother and father are not Christians; they are atheists.

'It means we believe Jesus was a really good man, but he wasn't the son of anybody who lived in the sky and made commandments,' said her mother. Katie's parents also used to be hippies.

'Jesus was sort of like the original hippie, wandering around in homemade hemp clothes with no real job.' There was something slightly unkind in Katie's father's voice, but she could tell he approved of this Jesus lifestyle.

'Not completely a hippie, more of an activist,' said her mother. She put her arm around Katie's father. 'A bit like us in our day, right, Jube?'

Jube, short for Jujube, they had told her when she was three. Short for chewy, colours-like-crayons, stick-in-your-molars sweets. Then, when she was seven, and more likely to understand the implications: 'Not really short for Jujube, honey, short for Jew-Boy. We're not Jewish, but your father would sometimes get discriminated against because of his looks.'

Jews were not Christians, and they were not atheists, although they also believed Jesus was just some guy. At seven, fully armed with implications, Katie had understood Jesus to be a tall man; he had a long dark curly beard with mashed-up jujubes stuck in it. He looked a little like her father, except he spoke more quietly, and his words had a certain sheen to them that made people listen. And now, at thirteen, Katie is being sent to a Baptist Church camp.

'Yep, we were activists in our day, all right,' said Katie's father.

They weren't very active now, though. Her mother worked three afternoons a week as a naturopath's assistant, and her father had recently retired, a condition Katie found unbearable. He bought a telescope and hung a map of the stars where the wall calendar used to be.

'Check this out, Kate,' he'd say, his eyeball fixed to the tiny end of the black tube. 'Far out.'

Her parents were old. They skittered around the house like dust bunnies. Mostly they left her alone, which was a good thing. Most of the time it was a good thing.

'They're a bunch of Bible-thumpers, though, Rick. Lots of conversions and carrying on. And she'll be on an island in Georgian Bay, for Chrissakes.' Katie's mother was lying on the floor in corpse position.

'Can't do her much harm. She's her own person. Besides, it's cheap and outdoors. She'll manage.' Katie's father looked up briefly from his telescope.

Katie stood in the doorway, wondering about conversions and how the fuck she would manage. So that was it, then. There were some things they were not going to tell her. They were just going to allow her to coast out into the world like that. Unprepared. She cleared her throat.

'It says on the list that the sleeping bag should be tightly wound in a groundsheet. That it should be waterproof.'

'Oh, man, they're exaggerating. Just stick it in this.' Her father left his constellations for long enough to pass her a Loblaws bag with a torn handle.

She had spent the next three evenings kneeling in her room, a piece of plastic she found in the tool shed spread underneath her like an ice rink, lengths of rope and bungee cord hooked and dangling from her fingers. The sleeping bag was old and army green, with a flannel camouflage-patterned lining. When she tried to roll it, the stuffing gathered in stubborn pockets. There were lumps that would not flatten. It took her three nights to force the thing into a more manageable shape. When it was finally finished, she placed the shining, self-contained parcel next to her dresser. It made the top of her skull jive with satisfaction when she woke up every morning and saw it waiting there.

The boat that is to take them over to the island is not a boat, it is a barge. Which means that it is used, mostly, for carrying cargo – a cargo of Christian campers in this case. A thin man with a large head is standing in the barge, waiting for the kids to hand him the suitcases they have lugged over from the underbelly of the bus. The barge is a rusty red colour, and looks, to Katie's citified eye, like the enlarged bottom of a milk carton, perfect for sailing on the rushing gutter waters of a spring thaw. She has her doubts about its reliability in the choppy expanse of bay adjoining the dock. But she follows the others, stepping down into the box, surrendering her bags to the skinny-big-head man. There is a narrow bench around the periphery; Katie finds a spot and leans against her sleeping bag, which she has decided to keep on her person for safe-keeping throughout the journey. A girl she recognizes from the bus sits down beside her and gestures towards the driver.

'That's Chris. Bit slow on the uptake sometimes, y'know? I mean, you can pretty much see the hamster running. Hockey hair, too. Bad scene.'

Hockey hair? Katie's own hamster is sprinting to catch up. But she does not want to fall behind – not now, when it seems there might be some crucial information in the offing. She had kept to herself on the bus to the marina, made sleepy and anti-social by the warmth and the uncomfortable fit of the situation. But now it is beginning to seem necessary, if she is to survive, to seek out clues, perhaps even an ally.

Chris wedges the last of the luggage into the space beneath the bow and starts the motor without a word to the human cargo. He is smiling, though. A good or bad sign? Katie cannot tell.

'This is your first year, right?'

Katie nods to the girl. The barge is now ka-chugging out into the waves, and she realizes she is disappointed by the lack of danger in its ponderous momentum.

'Good job with the groundsheet. Last year they, like, threw them overboard to test them.' The girl pokes at Katie's sleeping bag. 'Where are you from?'

'Toronto.' They threw the sleeping bags overboard? Katie feels a rush of vindication.

'I know, but what part?' The girl has raised her voice.

In exasperation? To compete with the wind? Either way, Katie does not want to risk losing her, this noticer of sleeping bags. 'Downtown, pretty much.'

'Lucky. I'm from Scarborough. *Scarberia*. My name's Tatyana. It's Russian. You can call me Tat, but not Tit or Tattie. I hate Tattie.'

'I'm Katie. How much longer?' The barge rises in slow motion on the swell of a larger vessel, then plonks down again on the other side. The islands look like fancy lady hats that have been tossed from the sky, the windswept pines sprouting like feathers from their edges.

'Ten minutes maybe. Then when we get in we'll have a welcome singalong and get cabin assignments. The singing's pretty good. I think Andy who teaches canoeing is coming back this year. Hottie. You should watch out for the snakes, though, the massasaugas. Poisonous rattlesnakes. I saw a huge one outside of A&C.' She looks meaningfully at Katie. 'That's arts and crafts.'

'Oh.' Katie gives an iffy laugh. She is trying to take cues, but Tatyana is so obliviously professional and offhand.

'I'm not joking. And they're endangered. So, basically, their lives are worth more than ours. If you see one – they look a little like fox snakes, and they do actually rattle – you have to report it immediately. Then the Parks people come and T&T them. Trap and tag.'

Katie is somewhat resistant to this synopsis of camp life. She changes the subject. 'I like your nose ring.' A small silver stud glints above Tatyana's left nostril.

'I like your barrette.' Tatyana reaches out and presses a finger to Katie's butterfly bobby pin, then leans in towards her. 'The other day I was on the bus and this guy sits down next to me, a pretty old guy, and he's being all creepy, checking me out, then he starts yelling at me. *Yelling.*'

Katie realizes Tatyana is waiting for something. Tatyana is waiting for her! 'No way.'

'Totally. He goes: *Congratulations, you slut! You are trapped. You are trapped in your world of demons and body mutilations. Congratulations!* Right in my face.'

'What did you do?'

'I had my compass in my pencil case, so I stabbed him with it just before I got off. Hard, in the leg.' Tatyana's voice is trembling.

Don't cry, thinks Katie. *Please don't cry.*

'Like, he might have been bleeding. But I didn't check.' Tatyana pokes at Katie's sleeping bag for the second time. But she does not look at Katie. Not for what seems like a long while.

Tatyana is waiting for me. 'Well,' Katie says, 'congratulations.'

'Yeah.' Tatyana raises her head and smiles. 'Congratulations.' And she gives the sleeping bag a little pat.

Tatyana and Katie stand on tiptoe, their backs to the cabin's large black window, their torsos twisted so they can see what is reflected there.

'My butt is so balloony in these pants.'

'Just wear a long shirt.' Katie is happy with the way her own butt looks, the cheeks nesting snugly behind each of the large back pockets of her jeans. She tugs at her belt loops, inclines her head to the side. This is the only way for them to get the full picture, perched outside on the rock that slopes steeply behind them to the water. The alternative is a makeup mirror clutched at arm's length, made to travel slowly down from head to hips.

Still, the window does not have the sharp-edged clarity of the real thing, and the shapes and shadows inside the cabin make an accurate image-reading impossible.

'Is that a smudge, or do I have something weird under my eye?' Tatyana turns to Katie.

'Smudge.'

They balance there, silently critiquing, for another few minutes, the rock bearing them impassively up, the sleek waters of the bay lip-lapping below.

'You know what I like about Andy, and maybe it's because he's older and everything, but he's really got a sense of *humour*, you know? I mean, his jokes are so not-stupid.'

Katie does know what Tatyana means: the way Andy's jokes are continuous and ironic, with none of the question-answer silliness she still, despite herself, finds funny and true. When Andy is joking he says, *There is something particular I know about this world and the people in it.* He speaks in peaks and valleys of wit, somehow absorbs the punchlines into his patter. It is grown-up, the way he jokes, which makes it seem ever-present and unattainable, like trying to take a snapshot of the atmosphere.

'Are you going to Bible Study?' Tatyana swats at a mosquito feeding on her forearm, then flicks the splayed body from her bloodstained skin.

The chapel is outdoors, on the tip of the island – two rows of logs for pews and a stone pulpit built so that the preacher stands against the backdrop of God's large unbroken sky. Katie and Tatyana sit on the second log from the back and nudge the wood-chips into tiny piles with their feet.

> *Love the Lord your God with all your heart*
> *And all your soul, and all your mind, a-a-a-and*
> *Love all mankind …*

There is always the singing.

'All mankind?' Tatyana whispers.

'All mankind.' Katie places her hand on Tatyana's knee in affirmation.

'What kind of man?'

'*All* kinds of *man*.'

'Congratulations.'

And they are off. To contain it, this blissful bubble that begins behind the breastbone, is inconceivable. But they are in chapel. Katie tightens her hold on Tatyana's knee, and Tatyana grabs hold of Katie's wrist. They squeeze each other and look straight into the face of the counsellor, who is quite pretty really, and has just finished reading from the Scripture, something about doling out bread or throwing stones.

I will not look at Tatyana. Katie is seized with the desire to do just that. *Now. No.*

On the log in front of her, she sees a heedful black head bobbing and knows it is Theo. Theo is one of the Ugandans, who are at the camp for free because they are refugees. His posture embarrasses her. And the way he is now quoting the Bible back, his English clipped and overly articulate.

'I think he's a believer,' says Tatyana.

'Mmm-hmm.' Katie still cannot look at her. Theo turns his head, blinks at them, his concentration fractured.

'Bi-zarre.' Tatyana sighs, overcome with responsibility or fatigue.

Katie also feels responsible; she wants to take Theo aside, teach him some sense of things here – what falls within the flimsy boundaries of the acceptable. Instead, she considers the counsellor, her well-scrubbed, sturdy certainty. And she thinks she wouldn't mind looking like that – sure of her place in the world. Still, she suspects Christianity would make her sluggish. The only other real Christian she knew was a babysitter she had for a few months while her mother was away in Australia on a walkabout. ('It means just what it says – we'll be walking about, absorbing the culture, the ways of life. Exploration, Kate, it's so essential.')

Katie loved the babysitter. Jan was strangely thin and wore clanky, sharp-edged jewellery, but made up for it by buying Katie miniature tea sets from the Chinese store up the street. At bedtime, she would read from a waxy blue book she pulled from her suede purse – Jesus stories, illustrated in brilliant comic-book hues. Sometimes the colours had been stamped slightly askew, so that the people appeared, literally, beside themselves. The lambs always seemed okay, though.

'You don't hate anybody, not really,' Jan said. 'You may dislike them strongly, but you don't hate them. Not truly.' From this Katie understood that, for Christians, feelings could be modulated and masked, turned up and down by the way you chose to name them.

Once, Katie had watched Jan help an old lady, a stranger, across the street. The lady was walking the way Katie did sometimes to drag out the minutes on the way home from school, placing her feet like decals on the street, edge to careful edge. 'Hurry up,' Katie had called, safe on the sidewalk, but Jan did not even look up. You had to be slow and helpful, always, if you wanted to feel Jesus' thick good blood moving inside you.

There are no showers at camp. Instead, there is morning dip. Which sounds like a popsicle, which is a good way to describe the way you feel during and after the thing itself. The girls stumble down the path, juggling unwieldy shampoo bottles and pink plastic soap dishes, hips enveloped in towels whose corners have been neatly tucked into the tight elastic at the waists of their bathing suits. The morning has not yet grown into itself; the air is cold and still holds the wearied swank of night. In the cove, the water is relatively calm, but further out, near Turtle Island, the waves are frothy, slightly malignant.

There is no escaping it; they slide in on the slick rock, hand over hand over hand along the dock, grasping for the next wooden board, the ice of Georgian Bay inching up their thighs, until, shoulders hunched high, they duck under, squealing. And when they come up, there is still the lathering and scrubbing to be done: step one, step two, with rinses in between, the soap lending a shimmering patina to the surface around them.

By the time the boys emerge from the trailhead, their hair pointing every which way like the rays of a kindergarten sun, the girls are back on shore, dripping, towels turbaned around their heads or clutched tightly around their shoulders.

'Do not even go near that thing,' Tatyana counsels as they pass the back of the lodge on their way to breakfast. She is referring to one of the only functioning machines at the camp, an ancient laundry wringer that leans up against the porch behind the kitchen. 'One guy once lost a whole hand.'

Katie can believe it; the wringer is the colour of an iceberg, and as bulky – it has the form and feel of disaster about it.

'But if you ever do get caught in it, there's a reverse button. You'd have to be pretty cool to find it, though, while your arm was being mashed. Do you see Andy up there?'

Katie has always known that there are dangers and there are antidotes, but knowing the antidotes doesn't ever seem to do anybody much good, really. You just have to hope and, if you are inclined, pray, that you can be cool, together, that you are, in some obscure way, *prepared*. She's not sure it is particularly helpful to dwell on the dangers – the snakes and the laundry wringers – for too long.

At breakfast, Katie and Tatyana are separated.

'What a total gyp,' says Tatyana. 'I'll meet you on the steps afterwards.'

Katie is seated at a table with Theo and a gaggle of girls from the youngest cabin. They are talking about snakes. Katie digs into her porridge, which is something she never thought she would like – it's a dirty white colour, homely and old-fashioned. But she does like it, hot, with brown sugar and just a splash of watery instant milk. It's the kind of food you can feel settle inside you. It comforts her.

'In Africa, the snakes are as big as my leg.' Theo seems to be addressing Katie.

One of the good/bad things about camp is that Katie can never tell when someone is having her on. It's best, when this happens, to feign interest in more practical matters. She digs deeper into her porridge, presses her spoon against a hard node of brown sugar.

'As big as my leg,' he repeats. He is definitely addressing Katie.

'Hmm,' she says, chewing energetically.

'Yes, you can run over a snake in your car, *ba-boom, ba-boom*, and the snake will still live.' He pauses.

Theo is waiting for me. 'Well …' Katie says.

'Yes, and if you look back, you will see the snake slide away into the jungle.'

'Slither, you mean.'

'Hmm?'

'Slither. Snakes don't slide, they slither.'

'No, the snake was sliding away.' He demonstrates on the table, sliding his arm along in an S formation, his hand the pretend head.

'Never mind.' Katie searches for and finds Tatyana, who is about to take a bite of toast, holding her mouth wide, teeth bared, so that her lipstick will not smudge. Katie tries to catch her eye, but there is too much commotion, what with the cutlery and the scraping of chairs. Soon they will sing the camp hymn and get on with their day.

'I hope you have a good morning, Katie,' says Theo.

'You have a good morning too, Theo,' Katie replies, surprising herself with her own formality.

'Yes.'

'K-Y-B-O,' Tatyana had instructed, on the way over on the barge, 'stands for Keep Your Bowels Open. There's a lot of stupid-ass codes and routines at this camp, but once you learn them you're basically set. There's no privacy in the kybe, so just be prepared to share your bodily functions.'

At first Katie couldn't stand it, the tacky violation of sitting side by side, your shorts pooled over your running shoes, the long pause before the piss hit – *plaap-plaap* – the reeking piles at the bottom, the boys (the boys!) eliminating frankly on the other side of the thin plywood separator. But now she doesn't mind so much, especially when Tatyana looks over at her and says, 'I gotta take a dump,' and they set off together, purposefully, down the trail. Today Henry, a nine-year-old loser from Quebec, follows them.

There are three seats in the kybo. Tatyana is partial to the middle one, because, she says, she feels less trapped. Katie chooses the one farthest from the wide-swinging door, where it is least likely she will be seen with the changing of the guard. They settle and wait. Henry begins to sing.

> *Yankee doodle went to town,*
> *Riding on a lady,*
> *Pulled her tits and made her shit*
> *And then she had a baby.*

'Too much orange drink at lunch,' says Katie.

> *When I die, bury me,*
> *Hang my balls on a cherry tree.*

If they crack, tabernac,
Send them back to Radio Shack.

'I lived in Montreal once,' says Tatyana and shifts on the seat.

'Parlay-voo?' says Katie. 'Shut-da-door.'

'It's "Je t'adore," and I'd appreciate you not being so immature.'

'Why'd you live in Montreal?'

'Oh, my mother. There was this guy who said he'd take us to the Caribbean on his sailboat, so we sold everything. I was going to take, like, correspondence courses. But he never showed. Well, he did, but he loaned the sailboat to some idiot Newfie. We stayed at his apartment for a while. He had these totally disgusting curtains. They were puke colour.'

'Oh.'

Henry has another verse.

Old MacDonald sitting on a bench,
Picking his balls with a monkey wrench.
Wrench got hot, burned his balls,
Peed all over his overalls.

Tatyana rolls her eyes. 'Loser!' she calls down through the space between her legs.

Henry makes farting noises.

Now Katie rolls her eyes at Tatyana, who shakes her head, then asks, 'How does a Newfie hitchhike in the rain?'

'How?'

Tatyana holds out her thumb, and with her other hand makes a little shelter overtop. 'Get it?'

'Oh, yeah,' says Katie, and reaches for the toilet paper, which unrolls with a soft conk against the wall at each rotation. But she doesn't really get it at all. She looks down at her feet, where two daddy-long-legs are performing a gangly pas de deux. Near the door, more tiny red spiders are scattered like an outbreak of

measles on the dun-coloured floor. The island is full of them:
spiders and snakes. She grabs for her shorts and stands up quickly,
zipping the fly. There are times when the things Tatyana says beg
questions, or a gesture meaning comfort, but something always
stops Katie. A compact private pride, or a realization that evapo-
rates when she tries to name it.

Tatyana pushes the door open. Henry is standing at the fork
in the path, doing a dance, half Indian chief, half chicken. Katie
gives him the finger.

'I forgot my bug spray in the cabin, you coming?' Tatyana is
asking. As if she needs to.

On the way down to the archery range, Katie begins to sing.

> We've got Christian lives to live,
> We've got Jesus' love to give,
> We've got nothing to hide
> Because in Him we abide.
> Love!

'In Him we abide?' Tatyana stops, frowns, starts up again, trips
over a root.

Katie rights her, brushes a pine needle off her knee. '"In Him
we live" is what it means.'

'"In Him we live?"'

'Yeah, Jesus is like a big container for us all, so we don't have
to worry about anything.'

'Congratulations, you are trapped,' says Tatyana.

They hold their breaths as they pass the kybo.

'Allow me to congratulate you,' Katie says, on the other side.

They link arms.

To get to the archery range you must cross over the blueberry flats, where the scrubby low bushes with their tiny round fruits offer some respite from the bare bulgy rock and hot sun. The trail markers are old but effective, their concrete bases and hot pink tips plainly pointing the way. Once past the flats, the terrain becomes marshy and treed; planks bridge the more moist parts of the path. The archery range is set up in a clearing next to a small bog, the targets nailed firmly to a row of spindly pines. The shade, the mulch, the mould and the humidity – all are ideal for the rapid reproduction of blood-sucking insects. The bugs are horrendous. They are like pieces of your brain broken free, vibrating violently close to your thin skin, demanding restitution.

'Archery is hell.'

'No, hell is a pyjama party in a toaster oven. This is purgatory.' Tatyana shoulders her bow expertly. But her aim sucks. She sends arrows hustling wildly into the woods, careening straight up into the clouds and zinging dangerously close to other humans on the range. One of them grazes the branch of a tree next to a mossy stump where Theo and his brother, John, are sitting.

'Can you get that, Kate?' Tatyana calls over her shoulder, already collecting her other misfires.

At Katie's approach, John looks up. 'I like your bugs,' he says, prodding at a glistening banana slug that is nosing its way forward through the mud.

'He likes your insects,' Theo agrees, getting up to lift the edge of a rock to expose a riot of potato bugs.

'Right,' says Katie. She bends to pick up the arrow, then turns her back on the boys.

Tatyana meets Katie halfway, winks at her. 'So?'

'They like our bugs.'

'I think they're orphans.'

Katie prepares to shoot. She is certain her aim is true, can in fact hear the cushioned splintering sound the arrow will make when it enters the target. The problem is in the letting go. Somehow she always ends up easing the string free, with none of the twanging necessary for a smooth and wilful trajectory. When she finally releases, the arrow, which is yellow and plastic, accented with synthetic orange feathers, falls limply to the forest floor.

'You are extremely bad at this.' Tatyana is crouched nearby, watching, her sweatshirt pulled up over her head in an attempt to block the bugs.

'Yes,' says Katie, only partway glum. 'Let's get out of here.'

They make a run for it while the counsellor is demonstrating what he claims is an ancient Iroquois bow position. To keep the mosquitoes at bay, the girls perform rapid karate chops in the air around their faces as they walk. Their breath comes quickly, in urgent puffs. It is unwise to talk in this state.

Back in the cabin, Tatyana reapplies her eyeliner, a fat navy blue streak across the top lids.

'Even?' She bends close to Katie, her eyes semi-closed like a lizard's.

'Yep.'

'Want some?' Tatyana spritzes some cologne on her neck. The room smells of counterfeit roses, DEET and maxi-pads.

'Just a bit.' Katie offers her wrists.

'Do you think Andy might be on in canoeing?'

Andy is on. He is very on. He gives a thumbs-up when he sees them coming over the ridge towards the boathouse, ignores the fact that they are not scheduled to be at the waterfront, sets them both up with paddles: 'No shorter than your chin, no taller than your nose.'

'I got ya,' says Tatyana, which even to Katie sounds pretty sorry.

'Okay, Kate?' Andy pokes her in the ribs. She opts for an emphatic nod.

Out on the water, they go to work.

'I like that shirt he's wearing, the way the sleeve's a bit ripped?' Katie is sterning; she switches to J-stroke, points them away from the weeds near the shore.

'Yeah, and excellent hair today, kind of mussed at the front.' Tatyana is an erratic paddler – usually she lily-dips distractedly, but there are times when it occurs to her to put some muscle into it. This is one of those times. Her paddle is scooping and churning heartily. They are moving at a fast clip out into the open.

Katie wonders if she should tell about the poke. It was a playful tease of a poke, but it hurt a little, and she has filed it in the realm of uninvited tickle. But she wants it to happen again, can imagine it happening again.

'Motorboat,' says Tatyana. 'Stop paddling.'

A squat grey-haired woman is helming the motorboat. She raises her hand to the girls as she roars by. They wave back, the canoe peaking and plunging over the wake.

'Did you see Andy's belt?' Maybe there is no need to bring up the poke.

'Mmm-hmm,' says Tatyana, trailing her fingers in the waves, 'a touch of class.' Then, 'Do you think he has a girlfriend in the city?'

'Probably. She's probably a waitress.' Katie mulls for a moment. 'With big tits and a pointy chin,' she adds recklessly.

'Yeeaaah.' Tatyana is now in full recline in the front of the canoe, and has stopped paddling entirely. 'I wish I was a waitress. I wish I was Andy's waitress.'

Katie stops paddling too, and gives the boat over to the rock and roll of Georgian Bay, gives herself over to the possibilities spindling out from that statement: *Andy's waitress.*

'Um, might be a good idea to start doing your job there, Skipper.' Tatyana is sitting upright and has placed the paddle across her knees in a position of readiness.

It's true; there is some action required of them. They have drifted around the point so that the dock is no longer in sight, and the wind has picked up. Katie turns the canoe around, which takes more vigour and force than she anticipated. Tatyana, too, has set to it with uncharacteristic diligence. They are moving forward, but slowly, the wind bullying them for no apparent reason. They are a bit of a joke, Katie thinks, in this limitlessness punctuated by the spiny protrusions of the Canadian Shield – two girls in a red fibreglass canoe, their lifejackets riding up like puffy straitjackets above their shoulders. She watches the straining in Tatyana's wrist as she pulls the blade of the paddle alongside the gunnel. What is it she notices there? A concentration, yes, but also a restrained jumpiness in the tendons. Fear. Tatyana is scared. And, oh, it frays at Katie's heart to see it. She paddles harder and begins to sing.

> *Go ahead and hate your neighbour,*
> *Go ahead and cheat a friend.*
> *Do it in the name of heaven,*
> *Justify it in the end.*
> *There won't be any trumpets blowin'*
> *Come the judgement day*
> *On the bloody morning af-tuh-uh-er ...*
> *One tin soldier rides away!*

By the time they reach the final verse, they can see Andy, who is bent over just below the treeline, to the left of the dock, single-handedly tipping the sludge out of one of the rowboats.

> *So the people cried in anger,*
> *'Mount your horses, draw your swords!'*
> *And they killed the mountain people,*

So they got their just reward.
There they stood beside the treasure,
On the mountain, dark and red,
Turned the stone and looked beneath it:
'Peace on earth' was all it said.

They are sad for a moment, and deep into themselves.

'That is a really good song.'

'I know.' Katie stops paddling. 'Do you believe in God?'

Tatyana turns and looks at her. 'Once, God answered my prayers. But once is not a fan-fucking-tastic record.' She pauses for a moment to rearrange the extra lifejacket she has placed as padding under her knees. 'And maybe once is not even a record. Maybe it's just once, y'know? I really wish we didn't have to have those powdered potatoes again for dinner.'

'Yeah,' says Katie, answering a question and a hope.

Because they have completed all the swim levels, Katie and Tatyana have been chosen as assistants to the swim instructor. Mostly, this means suntanning on the dock and blowing the whistle (one long blast) if they see any water snakes in the area. It seems conceited and laughable to Katie that the water has been cordoned off the way it has, the blue and white buoys bobbing ineptly in a line across the cove, a hawk coasting above. It is so different from the pool in the city, which smells of sterility and organization and is divided into two clear sections: the first for the novices and old ladies, the second for the real swimmers in their proud lines, who putter and slice, knowing exactly where to go and when to turn, even when they're on their backs. At camp, the bottom of the swimming area is uneven, unmarked, at times unknowable.

'I thought there might be baptisms,' says Katie to Tatyana. 'It would be good if there were baptisms.'

'Ugh. They force you under, you know.'

'Yeah, but when you come up, it's like you're someone else – congratulations! – you're totally transformed.'

'I will never let anyone push my head underwater.' Tatyana snaps the bottom of her bathing suit into place over her butt and passes Katie the suntan lotion.

'I would, I think. I think I would do it.'

There is a boy standing underwater. From the dock, Tatyana and Katie can see him. He is not swimming or floating, just standing. Not even moving, but being stirred somewhat by the currents and eddies of the water, his hands waving languidly at his sides, his turquoise swim trunks ballooning around his waist like some alien form of underwater vegetation. But there are no lilies or weeds in the swimming area; he stands alone, without shadow, and although the water is not entirely transparent – tiny bits of the bay hang suspended around him – the lines of his body are clear, only mildly distorted.

'I think that's Theo's brother,' says Tatyana, and they both watch as several empty marble-sized balls stream up from his mouth like the circles leading to a thought in a comic strip.

Maybe he wants to live down there, is what Katie thinks.

'I think we better tell Sue,' is what Tatyana says.

Sue is the swim instructor. She is at the far end of the dock preparing to demonstrate a dive, her toes curled over the edge, chin tucked to chest, head nestled between arms.

'He said he could swim,' she says, when Tatyana points. Then again, when she spots him, 'He said he could swim.'

They stand there, Sue and the girls on the dock, the boy in the water. Until something seizes Sue's features, and she takes a calm, uncanny stride from the dock, into the air and down into the cove.

Maybe John wants to live down there. The thought comes again, adamant and elementary. It does not seem a strange thought to

Katie – he looked so natural, and only moderately bewitched, more grounded in the water than on the ground.

Sue has pulled the boy up onto the rock that passes for a beach, where he begins to spit and snot, and then to cry. She clutches his head in her lap, holds him like that till she remembers her role, then shakes him free, her hands taking inventory of his body, checking for broken bones, prodding for bruises.

Not likely you'd get bruised underwater.

Through it all John does not speak, only stares appraisingly up at Sue, his swim trunks now glomming on to his thin legs.

Then Theo is there, wrapping a towel, then his own body, around his brother, enclosing him efficiently.

It says here that the sleeping bag should be wrapped in a ground-sheet. That it should be waterproof.

Katie watches them, stuck together on the rock like a pair of barnacles. She puts her arm around Tatyana, who leans into her. Before he leads his brother away to the cabin, Theo turns towards Katie and Tatyana and gives an official nod.

'He totally likes you,' says Tatyana.

'Whatever.' Katie sweeps her gaze along the cliffside on the other side of the cove, above the diving raft, where a sign has been posted. *No cliff-jumping.* Then she scans the murky distance of the water between.

Which is when she sees it – a disturbance near the buoys, a bulge and trail on the surface of the water. She blows the whistle, long and hard, so that Tatyana springs away from her, hands clamped over her ears.

'Snake,' she says. 'There's a snake.'

But, of course, there is no snake. What Katie saw – the clever, quick, limbless creature – is gone.

'I think you girls should go get dried off.' Sue takes the whistle from Katie's hand.

'No kidding,' says Tatyana, and grabs her goggles from the dock.

'Nice colour combo.' Tatyana points to Katie's gimp bracelet.

'Uh-huh, how's the cowboy?'

Tatyana is working on a piece of copper tooling. The mould is a man on a horse with a lasso.

'Not great.' She holds the copper up to her face to check her lipstick. 'Let's get some seed beads and go outside.'

On their way out of the craft cabin, they run into Andy.

'Whoa, girls.' He holds out a hand, and with the other hand smooths at something below his lip. 'Where's the fire?'

'No fire,' says Katie, 'just seed beads.'

'Cool necklace,' says Tatyana, reaching up to touch the wooden beads at his throat.

'Mmm-hmm.' He catches her hand in his and rubs his thumb along her wrist. 'See you in boating.'

'Okay,' says Tatyana.

'Bye,' says Katie.

The rock outside is grey and fissured, except where it is green with moss and multicoloured with bits of colour caught, incongruous, in the cracks.

'Do you think they could ever clean up all of these?' Katie licks her finger and presses it to two tiny beads, a red and a black, then brings them up to her face to examine.

'It would take infinity.'

Katie decides to ignore the fact that Tatyana is sniffing at the place on her wrist where Andy's thumb rub happened. 'It doesn't feel like a Saturday today. It feels like a ... a Wednesday.' She pushes down on the moss by her knee. 'It's like teeny, squishy toy trees.'

'What?'

'The moss.' Katie opens her pill bottle full of beads, pressing the lid down and to the side. 'Childproof,' she says, and pours some of the contents out into the lid, then pulls a piece of fishing line from her pocket. *Green then two blues then a yellow. Whole parades of shades.*

'I don't feel like beading,' says Tatyana, and lies back on the rock.

It is hot, and soon, after she has completed six cycles of colour for her bracelet, Katie lies back too. The day feels like a really good memory that is somehow happening in the present. She closes her eyes and stretches her arms out to the side.

'Y'know those small girls in canoeing?' Tatyana prods Katie with her foot.

Katie knows. 'They're all like *hee, hee, hee.*'

'Mmm,' says Tatyana, 'the small girls.' She lobs the lid of her pill bottle at Katie.

'Hey.' Katie lobs it back.

Tatyana picks it up and holds it in the air above them. The sun is clear and strong on their faces. 'My mom used to make me help her count her pills. Ever since I was a kid. It was a game.' She places the lid carefully on her stomach, and they both watch as it rises and falls in time with her breath. 'She'd slide them across the coffee table, one at a time. It's probably how I learned to count.' She grabs onto the lid and places it on Katie's stomach. 'Then she ODed. Code for overdose.'

'I know,' says Katie, too quickly. *I said it too quickly.*

'While she was in the hospital all these people came over. They made me carry this tray of tiny sandwiches around. They made me carry a fucking tray. And I was the one who counted the pills.'

Katie is sweating. 'But she's okay now, right?'

'Yep, she's okay. She thinks sending me here will put the fear of God in me.'

82

'Huh. Fear of God.' It seems to Katie that God is pretty much the last person anyone should be scared of.

Tatyana is singing to herself, softly.

> *Seek ye first the kingdom of God, and his righteous-neh-ess,*
> *And all these things shall be added onto you.*

Katie joins in for the hallelujahs, like an opera star, only with less volume and drama since it is past lights out.

> *Ah-ley-lou, ah-ley-lou-ou-yah!*

'Yah,' Tatyana repeats, 'ah-ley-lou-*yah*.' She swings her legs over the side of the bunk.

Katie studies the shape of the feet swinging above her – curvy, with narrow waist-like insteps and dirty blobs for the pads of the toes, heels and balls, just visible in the light sputtering through the window from the trail.

'Come up here, I really have to tell you something,' Tatyana whispers through the space between the bunks.

'Yah,' Katie says absently, and pushes on Tatyana's ankle so that her foot balances back and forth.

'I mean, *really*.' Tatyana pulls her feet up and dangles her head down instead. 'This is major, Katie.'

Katie nods and hoists herself up onto the top level.

'Okay,' she says once both her legs have made it, 'but I get the wall side. If you get all hyper, you're totally gonna push me out.'

'Whatever,' says Tatyana, and rearranges herself in showy accommodation. 'So what happened is – guess what happened! I made out with Andy! It was so weird, and it just happened while you were in the kybe brushing your teeth ... '

'No *way*. What do you mean you *made out*? What *happened*?' Katie is genuinely pleased and curious, and feels only a light fizz of jealousy at the back of her throat. She knows it is hers too, this making out. It is theirs, hers and Tatyana's, together. She snuggles down on the pillow so that their heads are even, so that the space between them is private and small.

'Well, he was just kind of walking with me towards the cabin, and then he had his hand on my back, well, kind of just above my butt, and we just started walking, and he's not really talking, and then we just stopped outside the maintenance cabin, and he bends down and his face is all like a nail brush when it touches my cheek, and he's got his tongue in my mouth so I kind of scream, but also stick out my tongue ... ' She stops for a second, furrows her brow, and, somehow, her cheeks end up furrowing too.

Katie understands how important it is to get them right, these details, the order of things. She reaches out and twists a piece of Tatyana's hair around her finger in encouragement.

'Yeah, we were frenching for a while. We'll probably sit together at campfire on Sunday. First we frenched, then he touched my boobs. French, boobs, french, boobs ... '

Tatyana doesn't really have much in the way of boobs, but she wears clingy shirts and is a little fat, so there is some bumpiness to her. Katie detests her own boobs; they look big even though they're not, and she thinks they should be more round, fold over a little. Instead they sit too low on her chest, with their strange puffy nipples that tip skyward like puppies' noses. Most days, she wears a tight undershirt over her bra to flatten them.

'Did he have a boner?' she says, and raises the sleeping bag into the air with her legs, so that her feet touch the rafters.

'Eww, you mean an *erection*?' Sometimes Tatyana could be all the Lady Prissy Superior.

'Congratulations,' says Katie, and then they are pitching from side to side, sliding on the narrow mattress, the laughter clasping at them in an unmanageable, marvellous way.

Tatyana is the first to slow her breath, to speak. 'I still think Theo likes you.' It is an attempt to bolster, to smooth some upset or imbalance between the two girls.

'Whatever – he freaks me out.' Katie shoves Tatyana's arm away, with less a laugh than a voiced smile, recycled. Why try to talk about *her*? Where is the point in it?

'I heard his parents got shot.' Tatyana's face is set in the same expression she uses sometimes while singing hymns, pure and put on. To be solemn so soon after laughter is a trespass. It is bringing Katie down. She suddenly knows she could punch Tatyana square in the nose, can feel the welcome contact, middle knuckle to begging, bull's-eye cartilage.

'Right in front of him. In the middle of the night, they just busted right in on them. He took his brother and hid behind the dresser. Jenny told me in A&C. Can you imagine?'

'No,' says Katie, meaning *I don't want to, don't make me.* 'I better go down.' She begins the slow clamber to her bed, then stops to waggle her tongue and spasm her groin.

'Fuck *off*,' says Tatyana, and Katie does.

Back on her own bunk, she hunkers down, her back to the world, nose pressed against a graffitied beam. She knows the words scrawled there by heart. *Sex is fun but use pertexion. Jesus loves me the most.* And, inexplicably: *Prince Charles was here and a good time was had by all*, a jagged crown doodled to the side. She has carved her own message above a whorled black knot in the wood: a large letter K, with a plus underneath, and a question mark below that, then a heart around the whole thing. Who is the question mark? *That's for me to know and you to find out.* She closes her eyes. There are flickering white amoebas against the maroony insides of her eyelids. *Shot*.

Could she imagine it? If she did, what would happen? When she was younger there were the nightmares, the witches who came roaring, perched high and ridiculous in glistening red tractors. And the trick, when she woke up in a daffy panic, was always to think it through, to think right through to the worst. The *worst*. She'd close her eyes and see it: herself, tied to the railway tracks, paralyzed, the head witch barrelling down the tracks in her tractor. Tracks? Tractor? It didn't matter. It was terrifying. And she would be crushed. This was the worst: the marrow squeezed out of her bones like toothpaste under those giant black rubber treads, her brain a smushed eggplant. And death would be what? Nothing to worry about. A blank. The witches could do as they might, mix her in with the newts and muddy bits of bat. She would feel nothing, be *nothing*.

But to not dream it, to have it there, unfolding in front of you, to the worst. Did it become a dream that you could never think through? *Shot*. And afterwards, to not be dead, to live and walk and talk – the dream that was never a dream in the first place dogging you through your nights.

'Are you asleep?'

'Yes.' Katie makes loud snoring noises.

'I'm coming down. Should I bring my nail polish?'

The raid was Katie's idea.

The girls stumble clumsily out onto the trail, pockets bulging, steps still sluggish with what they have seen. There is only half a moon in the sky, but it is iridescent and high. Katie's father liked to talk about the moon. 'Some people believe the moon was once part of the earth, Kate, that it was flung off when the world was first forming. Now it just hangs out – waiting, waxing, waning, watching – caught in orbit.' Katie wants to be in her bed, and she wants to be anywhere but in her bed. In orbit, maybe. Today is Saturday, and tomorrow is Sunday.

Tatyana is piecing something together, Katie can tell by the increasing confidence in her stride. *Let's not. It was my idea.*

'Theo's brother, John,' says Tatyana wonderingly, 'sleeps with his eyes open.'

Sunday mornings at camp are relaxed. The bell does not ring until eight-thirty, and there is sometimes French toast for breakfast. But chapel is serious business. The director, a giddy, God-filled woman, becomes sombre, more director-like. She tells them what they should do, according to the Lord. Then they sing.

> *Jesus is the rock of my salvation,*
> *His banner over me is love.*
> *Jesus is the rock of my salvation,*
> *His banner over me is love.*
> *Jesus is the rock of my salvation,*
> *His banner over me is love,*
> *His banner … over me-ee … is love!*

There are actions to the song: a waving motion in the air above their heads on *banner*, and a hand placed over the heart on *love*. The director's long necklace swings wide while she sings, then moors itself to one of her large breasts. After the singing is done with, the campers are sent, with their paperback Bibles, to sit on the point and read about Jesus. This will help them prepare a place for Him in their hearts.

Katie and Tatyana find a spot behind a boulder and sit back to back. It is forbidden to talk.

Katie flips through her Bible, then squints up at the sky. The day is a milky tea colour, clouds steeping in the sun's dull rays.

The reflection on the water is causing a slow, slightly stupefying pulse behind her eyebrows. She can feel her friend's ribcage against her own, can sense Tatyana's breathing becoming deep and regular. She fans through the Bible again, then jabs randomly at a page with her finger.

Under Mark, and the subheading 'A Dead Girl and a Sick Woman,' she finds the following passage:

> *He did not let anyone follow him except Peter, James and John the brother of James. When they came to the home of the synagogue ruler, Jesus saw a commotion, with people crying and wailing loudly. He went in and said to them, 'Why all this commotion and wailing? The child is not dead but asleep.' But they laughed at him. After he put them all out, he took the child's father and mother and the disciples who were with him, and went to where the child was. He took her by the hand and said to her, 'Talitha koum!' (which means, 'Little girl, I say to you, get up!'). Immediately the girl stood up and walked around (she was twelve years old). At this they were completely astonished. He gave strict orders not to let anyone know about this, and told them to give her something to eat.*

Katie shuts the book, sets it down on the rock beside her, then closes her eyes. Grogginess and the glare of the day have made her credulous. They should give the girl porridge, she thinks.

> *Fire's burning, fire's burning,*
> *Draw nearer, draw nearer,*
> *In the gloaming, in the gloaming,*
> *Come sing and be merry.*

What is the gloaming, anyway? Katie shifts on the rock. She and Tatyana have positioned themselves at the edge of the crowd, close to the campfire, so they can observe the counsellors but also take off early if things get tedious. Katie is unhappy, though she cannot say exactly why. The campfire is raging and hot, and soon the stars will pierce finely through the blackness above, but the sunset was torrid, the clouds like slabs of bloody meat slapped up against the darkening sky. And there is something irritating about the night closing in around their little circle lit by fire, something duplicitous about this makeshift family.

She feels far away from everything.

And she misses her parents quite utterly. Her father, first thing on a Sunday morning, frying pan in hand: 'Sun up, or over easy, little woman? The early birds do not get the tofu, is what I say. Don't tell your mom.' They'd sit across from each other, the yellow yolk leaking out onto their plates, their toast spears dripping, and share a cup of coffee. Her mother, in her purple caftan, squatting in the garden: 'I want it to look completely chaotic, sweet pea – lots of unplanned variety.' She'd toss the seeds in the air and pull Katie to her breast in a hugging dance, a sweet stain of soil on her cheek, her eyes blank as a baby's. Afterwards Katie would pick up the trowel and straighten things out a little, because too much chaos, she knew, could be a bad thing.

'Jee-sus, the bugs are bad,' she exclaims, to keep herself from crying.

Theo, who is sitting a few feet away, deeper in the crowd, looks over at her and frowns.

Who does he think he is, with his tight brown skin and kinky hair?

'Here,' says Tatyana, and passes her some Muskol, but does not look at her. She is trying to locate Andy, who does not seem to be among the group at the front.

Katie is going to cry anyway. They are singing the campfire song again, this time in rounds. She elbows Tatyana. 'What does *gloaming* mean?'

'Now, *now* is the gloaming,' Tatyana says distractedly.

Now is the gloaming.

Tatyana has spotted something in the woods; she has risen onto her knees and is straining to see. Katie also rises to get a better view. Near the boathouse, two people are standing, the taller one inclined towards the shorter one. Katie recognizes Andy by his bell-shaped Gilligan hat, but she cannot make out the other person. Until the short person lifts her head to kiss the tall person.

'Sue,' Tatyana whispers, and rocks back on her heels.

'Are you sure?' But Katie herself is sure. The world is nothing but a big, round fucked-up place, all the way from Scarborough to Uganda. She reaches out to her friend.

Tatyana shakes off Katie's hand like a dog shaking off water. Then she grins wide. 'They better not make us do that asshole round again.'

In the morning, Tatyana will not get out of bed. In fact, she will not move.

'I say to you, get up,' Katie whispers, and places her hand ceremoniously on Tatyana's shoulder.

The shoulder quavers and Katie hears a horking sound from the vicinity of the head. She bends closer. 'Congratulations,' she calls softly into the opening of the sleeping bag.

'Do not fucking touch me. And don't let anybody see me. Especially Andy. *Especially* Andy.'

'It's just a small bite, I'm sure it will go down soon. You can wear pants.'

Tatyana's leg, from the knee down, has ballooned drastically, the skin blotched and generally distressed-looking.

'Probably a spider,' the camp nurse had said while slathering calamine on Tatyana's calf the night before. 'Take an antihistamine and rest for a while.'

Katie has a hard time believing in calamine lotion; the colour is so phony, and it dries like kindergarten paint on the skin. Still, Tatyana had seemed relieved at the time, and hobbled heroically back to the cabin.

'You can probably get out of morning dip.' Katie strokes the shoulder tentatively.

'I *hate* myself. You don't know anything about me.'

You don't hate anybody, not really. You may dislike them strongly, but you don't hate them. Not truly.

'Just leave, please.'

'I could bring you some toast.'

'Just leave.'

Out on the trail, Katie passes several girls from her cabin coming back from the waterfront. She stops one of them. 'Did I miss morning dip?'

'Yeah, I think Sue left.' The girl shakes her head, and her towel turban slumps to the side. 'You might be able to catch her.' She shivers and raises her eyebrows doubtfully.

The reek from the kybo is particularly bad this morning – the mild aroma of kids' shit undercut sharply by ammonia. Katie hurries past, but the smell follows. It is in her throat. Just before she reaches the lodge, she hears something in the bushes: a rattling. And when she looks, there is movement. A snake? No, only a pile of dry leaves made rowdy by the wind.

At least snakes had the decency to give a warning, and they weren't really evil, no matter what the Bible had to say. Snakes were just *snakes*. And spiders, though sneaky, were also just doing their thing. It was people you had to look out for. They had whole histories and prehistories wrapped up in their heads, whole continents heaving and shifting inside of them that could erupt without warning. Without any warning at all. *Why all this commotion and wailing? The child is not dead but asleep.* And where was Jesus, the pushy, water-walking magician, when you really needed him?

Morning dip is over. There is no sign of Sue, or anyone else for that matter. The sun is poised midway up the flagpole on the point. The wind and water seem friendly, at ease with each other. The morning is glorious. Katie turns to go back to the cabin, shampoo still in hand. At the far, marshy end of the cove, someone is bending towards the water. Katie walks to the trailhead and peers over the woodpile to get a closer look. It is Theo, intent on something bobbing in the waves. She moves closer, pushing her way through clinging brush, her shampoo now wedged in her armpit.

'Good morning, Katie,' says Theo, without disturbing his focus on the bobbing thing.

'Morning,' she says, stepping out into a narrow muddy space on the shore.

'I'm trying to save the frog.' Theo has extended a long hooked stick above the surface of the water and is now slapping it fitfully just in front of the frog, as if trying to get its attention.

But it is not a frog, really. It is several frogs, Katie thinks, feeding on something, and making a terrible, hungry gasping sound. She squints and steps closer. But where are the heads? She counts six fused legs – or are they tentacles? – two gaping maws, but no distinguishable heads. The freaky not-really-a-frog is spiralling in the water, unable to coordinate a kick in any one direction. It is horrifying to watch. Katie brings her hand to her mouth, but does not look away.

'Maybe if you hold on to my hand, I could stretch out…' Theo is intent on rescue.

Katie shakes her head and gestures towards the creature. 'God made that.'

Theo glances up at her, then jerks his head towards the horizon. 'Then He made that, too.'

The sky is full of light, the clouds daubed and sectioned with new sun. It sounds silly, but it's the truth: the waves are *dancing* around the rocky shores of the island. For the first time, Katie understands that it is possible to feel two or more completely opposite things at once. She wants very badly to believe, and at the same time, knows that she cannot. And knows that the wanting to believe leaves a gap in her … in her what? In her soul? It makes her angry: to feel, then to itemize her feelings, then to be no closer to a solution. And because Katie's feelings are sometimes, but not always, played out in her actions, she takes the stick from Theo, leans far over the water and pushes the bungled frog out into the weeds, where it soon becomes tangled and tired of the struggle.

REFUSE

Smack dab in the muggy depths of summer, in the midst of an ornery garbage strike, Oldrick Pietraszek was forced to dismantle his air-conditioning unit.

'I don't think that's a good idea,' said his best friend, Steeney.

'We'll lend you a fan,' said Ravi.

'You'll choke to death in there,' said his ex, Alice.

'It's probably not just that,' said Steeney. 'You just need to try a different ointment. Or acupuncture.'

Oldrick's hands had hardened, reddened and cracked like clay across his knuckles.

'Eczema is stress-related,' said Lynn. 'Go running, or do some of that sweaty yoga. What's it called, Ravi? Right, *bikram*. Do some of that.'

'Air conditioning is primo essential,' said Steeney. 'You're loco to shut it down.'

But Oldrick had heard that sometimes the mould and bits of mildew stuck in these contraptions could cause allergies, immune deficiencies, fragile moods and mental states. And when it was off, his hands seemed to itch and ooze less, although his nights were shot through with whispery insomniac visions and his sheets weighed against his thighs like large dry leaves of gyproc. It was too hot, really.

Oldrick's apartment was located above a coffee shop called the Human Bean. The Human Bean used fair trade and community-development initiatives to create equitable partnerships with coffee-growing outfits in South America and Africa. The café's walls had been painted a deep pumpkin colour, then sponged over with a still deeper pumpkin, with the baseboards and other accents in a pure white. Mugs of all shapes and sizes lined a narrow royal-blue shelf along the south wall. Above the mugs was a cheery sign: *Bring your own! Use your own!* Next to this was a bulletin board with more messages, both hand-drawn and computer-generated: *For yoga with Joy, For sale, For a cleaner karma, For rent, Forgive me!, Forests are forever, Forget about* GMO. The people in the café were chatty or morose. They chose their tables, pulled books out of bags and played with their teaspoons. There were grandmotherly lesbians, young moms in sloppy tank tops with cumbersome strollers and young moms in capris and crop tops with marathon strollers. Although it was August, several lone men with ratty copies of Rilke tucked in their back pockets shivered rapturously in the corners. Against the north wall, on another royal-blue shelf, jars of precious beans with names like Sumatran Surprise, Zambian Zing or Mellow Morn were perched. The beans were beautiful burnished pods in more shades of brown than Oldrick would have thought possible, and like shiny beads or marbles, they begged to be rolled appraisingly between thumb and forefinger. And the smell – the richness of the earth and the raging heat of the fire, elemental and good.

The servers were pierced and philosophical. 'Oh,' they might mutter, 'you'll have to wait a long time for that cappuccino, but you know *how it is* …' Or, with thumbs hooked through their belt loops, 'You can pay for that, um, whenever …' Late at night when they were closing up, Oldrick could hear their music through his hardwood floor. Joni Mitchell, with her trills and sweet triumphs of conscience, before she got hard and mad at record execs and the washed-up world that spawned them. Or happy hip hop to mop floors to. Sometimes, if he was trying to concentrate or watch TV, he would go down and wave to the servers through the glass, then mouth apologetically, 'Could you maybe just lower the bass a bit?' And they would nod at him, or give funny little mock salutes, then skip over to turn it down a notch.

In the eight months since he and Alice had split, Oldrick had quit his job and cashed three savings bonds, in the hope of completing something, a piece of art. It was to be a work both sorrowful and complex, but in no way souped up with the detritus of his surroundings. He wanted it to come – and this he admitted without any of the semi-bashful self-consciousness of most of his peers – *from a deep place*. On the Monday night after he shut down his air conditioner, he stretched a new canvas and prepared a palette. The apartment was clean: tub scrubbed, dishes washed, clothes wedged in hamper. Inspiration was imminent. Then the music began. It was a familiar melody, but the melody itself seemed to be trailing a distant second to the backbone beat of the tune, which pulsated persistently up from downstairs. Oldrick put down his brush and prepared for a polite exchange with the Human Bean's server of the hour. On the way down the stairs, he practised a wince-like, reluctant face, and rehearsed orders masquerading as polite pleas: *I actually have this album, Just as a courtesy, Not the volume exactly, Hey neighbour, I guess the insulation's not so hot* ... But when he peered inside the café, he could see no one. It was possible they had closed up and forgotten to flip the switch on the stereo. He knocked loudly on the door, feeling silly and unmannerly. Nothing. He knocked again. Still nothing. And then movement from the direction of the basement, movement that turned out to be a broom handle attached to a thin, tufty-headed boy/man of about twenty Oldrick had never seen before. He waved to the new server and went through his wincing charade. The tufty head was now in full view; he had twirled the broom handle around and was balancing it on one end in his palm like a circus performer, weaving back and forth in a concentrated crouch in order to keep the stick upright. He wove right past Oldrick and managed a nod before the broom handle crashed to the floor.

'Could you turn the music down a little?' Oldrick mimed the twisting of a volume knob.

The coffee guy smiled and tapped at his watch. 'We're closed,' he replied congenially. Or at least Oldrick suspected this was what he said.

'Music,' Oldrick yelled, and plugged his ears in a slightly exaggerated fashion. 'Too loud!'

Then the coffee guy did something unexpected. He made a face at Oldrick. It was the kind of face people make instinctively, without inhibition or remorse, when ire rises in them like acid. It was the physical equivalent of a spoken *so what?*, laced with revulsion. And it scared Oldrick because it made him want very badly to punch the coffee guy.

On Tuesday afternoon Steeney came by to invite him to a dinner party at Ravi and Lynn's. He walked her downstairs, where they found a dog sitting on the stoop, his lead tied to Oldrick's mailbox. It was an old, snarly dog, with a cranky expression, and when Oldrick bent down and held out his hand so it could sniff, it curled its lip and strained away, so that for a second the bottom of the mailbox pulled away from the wall where it was anchored.

'Demon dog,' said Steeney. 'Does that happen a lot?'

Oldrick nodded, then walked her to her car, whose back seat was littered with the small white foamy turds used in packing crates and kindergarten projects.

'You transporting something?' He pointed to the foam.

'No, I just like them. And just in case I have to move, y'know?' She ran a finger across one of her eyebrows. 'Sweaty.'

Oldrick nodded.

Steeney managed a sympathetic look despite her perspiration. 'James will be there.' She punched him on the shoulder. 'All hands on deck.'

When Oldrick arrived at Ravi and Lynn's, the table was already set, and Alice was already seated.

'This is James,' she said, motioning towards someone coming from the direction of the kitchen with drinks in hand. Oldrick took him in, but blinkingly. He saw the way James's fingers curled cleanly and possessively around the two tumblers he held, he saw that James's chin was somewhat weak under his reddish beard, and he noticed James's belt, or more specifically, James's belt buckle, which had the look of an oversized forged foreign coin. *There is no way*, he thought, just like that, and at the same time he sensed how easy and odd it was to be in the same room with her.

We are still together, he thought. *We are still the same.* It was as obvious to him as James's belt buckle.

James released the tumblers gently next to Alice's placemat. 'Good to finally meet you,' he said, and held out his hand.

There are many means for people to greet one another, and these means vary according to region, intimacy and intoxication level. Oldrick knew this, but this hand, extended like a limp cold-cut, struck him as droll, out of context. It was the suburbs of Paris, 1986. He had been seventeen, an exchange student and miserably out of his element, and his French counterpart a snooty, almost Olympic swimmer. Oldrick had gone to meet him one day and had had to endure a line of high-breasted, racer-backed Gallic beauties as they hauled themselves smoothly onto the deck, then tilted in, wry, wet and accomplished, for the required cheek-to-cheek-to-cheek-to-cheek kiss. His bronchioles had constricted while his blood flew in a great flock to his groin.

He had no idea what to do.

Ravi came in carrying a thick white china bowl that smelled of lemons and cheese. 'Risotto,' he said, and leaned over to place the bowl in the centre of the table. 'You need to always be aware of the stirring, isn't it?'

Isn't it? was Ravi's trademark. It had started out as an ESL thing and evolved into an affectation. Oldrick liked it.

The doorbell rang and it was Steeney, then Lynn's brother Jack with a kalanchoe plant.

'Those things last forever,' said James. 'Impossible to kill.'

'Really?' said Steeney. 'On mine the leaves always go brown and crispy.'

'Oh, sure, but it never dies.'

What a nob.

Oldrick found Lynn in the kitchen with a tiny slug.

'It was on the spinach. Do you believe it?'

Oldrick did.

She poured some red wine into a deep long-stemmed glass and handed it to him. 'I think you should turn it back on, Olds. Just deal with the scabby hands.'

'It's more that I notice a different kind of racket now without the whirring. Can I help you with that?' He took the salad bowl and plucked some tongs from the wall where they hung.

'It's a Thai dressing. We went a bit multiculti, isn't it?' She smiled.

At the table there was talk of conflict and post-colonialism. Ravi got freaky and accused Lynn of loose morals around notions of terrorism.

'You mean I'm an ethical slut?' She plunked her dessert fork down on the table.

'I think that's a book,' said Steeney. 'I think I read that.'

'Different emphasis,' Oldrick whispered.

'Oh,' she said. Then, with an urgent nod, '*Right*.'

'You can't just foist your view on someone when they are not primed or prepared to accept it, and expect them to sit back and take it without some, well, repercussions. When people feel helpless and politically inarticulate, they have to *act*.' Lynn was stabbing the fork gently but emphatically into her open palm.

'That's the role of education. Stop with the fork,' Jack said. 'Did you make a dessert that requires small forks?'

'Education's for the birds. It's just another form of cultural imperialism. Tofu cheesecake. Just in case it's dairy that's making Olds's hands flare.'

'The risotto had cheese.' Ravi shrugged. 'And cream.' He shrugged again.

Lynn went over to pick up the baby, Nathalie, who lay fussing on a fine fleecy blanket on the living room floor. Ravi watched Lynn as she made her arm like a shovel, scooped Nathalie in close and stroked her until she began to coo and trill. 'Woo, war hawk,' he said, and whistled through his teeth.

'You get educated,' Lynn said, hip jutted, jouncing, 'you learn to couch all your true beliefs in jingoistic jazz. You lose your essence, really …'

'You're talking garbage, Lynn.' Jack rocked onto the back legs of his chair and balanced there, waiting.

But Lynn was staring at Nathalie, who was staring back.

'Speaking of garbage, this strike smells, isn't it? What are you doing with yours, Olds?' said Ravi.

'He's not doing anything and they boarded up his fire escape for soundproofing,' Steeney said.

'Who?' said Jack.

'That's dangerous,' said Alice.

'Probably illegal,' said James.

'We're going to the dump on Tuesday. Just leave your bags out front. We'll drop them off, right, Rav?' said Lynn.

'Tuesday. Where's the cheesecake?' Ravi made a face and pulled his napkin off his lap like a bullfighter, which made Steeney laugh and James frown.

'Don't forget the coulis,' called Lynn.

The coulis was raspberry, and its colour filled Oldrick with a simple, solid happiness.

'How's your art?' said Jack.

'Good, it's good. I'm going for something, um, uncluttered.'

'What?' said Alice.

Oldrick stared hard at the coulis. Lately all he could manage were caricatured head shots of celebrities with old-fashioned matchboxes stuck up their noses.

'All good caricatures have their roots in rage,' said Steeney, who sometimes wore her smarts on her sleeve.

'You're doing caricatures?' said Alice.

'In the evenings,' said Oldrick. 'Do you spoon this directly overtop?' He pointed at his cheesecake.

Steeney drove him home through the heavy night. With the windows open, the air moved slightly, but the smell was worse. Mounds of refuse were piling up on street corners, and heavy-haunched raccoons had begun their stealth work. Outside Oldrick's apartment, it was slapstick waiting to happen. Three splayed banana peels and a toppled toaster with jam smeared on its sides rested unassumingly on the sidewalk.

Steeney sighed. 'That café you live above is so cute. Kind of like the show where the friends all live together?'

'It's called *Friends*, Steeney.'

'Sorry.'

'It's okay.' He hugged her. 'I'll see you soon.'

On Monday, Oldrick began a painting titled *Woolworth's Etc.*, then abandoned it and made himself a grilled cheese sandwich.

On Tuesday, Steeney came by to tell Oldrick her dream.

'See, I'm in this taxi cab, with too many people, and the taxi cab is speeding down a large street that may be a highway. No, it's not a highway, it's definitely a wide street. The people in the taxi cab are arguing and laughing.' Steeney stubbed out her herbal cigarette, dabbed at her forehead with the bottom of her T-shirt and leaned in close to Oldrick. 'I'm pretty sure we're on our way home from a party. I'm certain that I've been drinking and want badly to be home. On the inside roof of the cab – the ceiling, I guess – a movie is playing, some sort of Beatles docudrama.'

'Beatles the band or – '

'The band. Anyway, up on the screen there's John, Paul, Ringo and George and they're all bopping open-mouthed in their stovepipe pants, then striding all close-mouthed and serious across a strawberry field. I can't stop watching this thing until the cab stops and we're at the airport. Which makes sense, really.'

Oldrick nodded.

'So, when I look out the window, I realize all the planes on the runway are made of that hard rock candy they import from some seaside town in England. But no one really seems to mind.'

'Did you get on one of the planes?'

'What?'

'Did you get on a plane?'

'That's not really the point.'

'Oh.'

Steeney got up and went into the kitchen to make some tea and Oldrick stayed behind and thought about dreams. *What did the dream mean?* was a question Oldrick did not often ask himself. Too regularly, he believed, dreams were treated as gaping gateways to self-analysis or tightly packed bundles of symbols substituted for the detailed and detonated stories of the day-to-day. He did not dis his own dreams; he bowed to them as he might to foreign dignitaries, directed them towards the hors d'oeuvres and then carried on with his own more domestic business.

Still, he thought he knew something of this dream of Steeney's. It reminded him of a memory, or a story someone had told him he'd only half listened to. Perhaps it was a daydream, or one of a series of images that had flashed before his mind's eye while he dozed on the subway or in a dentist's waiting room. It might even have been a movie. In his version he always ended up at a loading dock on the water, with boxes and shipping crates piled high on all sides. He was in a crowd, and beneath the sound of the laughter of the people around him, who had spilled out into the spaces between the stacked cargo, he could hear a thin wailing that made him want first to flee and then to sleep. But no one else seemed aware of the terrible sound. They were passing around a mickey of gin and a crumpled pack of cigarettes.

Oldrick had no choice but to seek out the source of the wailing. He pushed aside some refrigerator-sized boxes, which seemed to him inappropriately light, and found his way into a clearing of sorts. Between a forklift and another fridge box stood a giant iron cage. Inside the cage was a young, very frightened buffalo. The beast's fur was wet, and, as he drew closer, Oldrick noticed that it was shivering. When he reached through the bars to touch the wet fur, the buffalo shuffled backwards, then resumed its keening. Oldrick pressed his face up against the cage. He wanted nothing more than to be able to comfort the creature, to hold its large shaggy head against his chest. He peered through the bars. 'Hey,' he said. The buffalo raised its eyes to meet his, and as it did, its wail became less like a cry and more like a song. It was the most melancholy and astonishing melody Oldrick had ever heard. He might have described it as otherworldly, but for its texture, which was so imperfect and full-bodied that it could only have earthly origins.

Steeney brought him a mug of green tea mixed with mint. The steam from the tea rose like a cipher, and through the window Oldrick watched a child on the street kicking a crushed can vehemently along the sidewalk. Then the doorbell rang.

'I'll get it,' said Steeney.

'No, no,' said Oldrick, 'it's probably for me.' He passed his tea to her as she followed him to the stairs.

It was the tufty-headed coffee guy, waving one of Oldrick's garbage bags high in the air. 'Is this yours, eh, buddy? IS THIS YOURS?'

Oldrick considered the coffee guy. Then he lied. 'No,' he said, and closed the door. Emotions were running high and he thought it would be for the best.

'Did you just lie?' Steeney passed him back his tea.

'I thought it would be for the best.' Oldrick scratched at his ring finger and it began to bleed. 'That guy doesn't like me.'

'Try this,' said Steeney. 'Imagine the guy like dust or dandruff on your T-shirt, and whenever the idea of him starts to bug you, just brush it off. But not just metaphorically. Really, physically.' She began to paw at his T-shirt sleeves. 'If you don't actually do it, it won't work. The idea of it is not enough.'

The next day dawned hot and slightly more humid than usual. Oldrick found a note in his mailbox. The note was carefully paper-clipped to one of his old phone bills. *This is proof*, read the note. *I could get you hauled down to the station with this. Just like in the Guthrie song. Arlo, not Woody*. The note was unsigned. Oldrick was not up on his Guthrie, so he used the internet.

Then Alice called.

'Did you know there's a protest song named after you?'

'You can get anything you want.'

'What?'

'At Alice's Restaurant.'

'That's the one.'

'It's really long. Like, hours. I just called to let you know James and I are moving in together. I thought you should know.'

'It's Arlo that sings it, not Woody.'

'I know. I'm sorry, Olds. I'm just ... How're your hands?'

'Handsome. I've gotta go. I'm doing something.'

There was a bad time before the good yet brief time before the end, when Alice was often angry, but angry like a pot boiled dry – nothing left to work with, really. They were arguing about something Oldrick had failed to do efficiently or on time: pay a bill or deliver old canvases to the local school's art centre to be recycled. Or they were dissecting Oldrick's jealousy, which, according to Alice, he stoked by shutting down, erecting force fields of self-satisfaction and satire. (What was it that Oldrick had been jealous of? Once, a man at the opposite table in a restaurant wearing a stupid plaid shirt and a face full of social-worky solace. Another time, Alice's mother's laugh, or, more specifically, the way Alice reacted to her mother's laugh, with her own, different-sounding laughter. Other incidents he could not remember; some he refused to remember. Others still, Oldrick suspected, fabricated by Alice.) Alice wanted to be reasonable, to discuss things using terms that neutralized, to locate the roots of feelings, to stop blaming. But he could not do it. Alice had a trick: she was able, even when she was not overtly indicting him, to make Oldrick seem the culprit.

They stood in the small rectangle of hallway from which the rooms of their apartment petalled out, bodies locked in casual postures of confrontation. Oldrick might even have been leaning against a door frame, as if at a college party. Alice was wearing jeans that were too short for her; Oldrick could see her faded pink socks slouching around her ankles. Her sweater was something cowl-necked and off-white that had been expensive but now had a certain mussiness to it that might have been remedied by a good dry cleaner. She was trying to grow her hair but hated it near her face. It was clipped up in a tangled sprout over her right ear with a small barrette that looked like a clothes peg.

'You are not listening to me and you are *so mean*.' She backed into the kitchen, keeping him in her sights as if he were a wild animal. Then she shook her head and he watched as her eyes widened slowly and emitted three small, fast-moving tears.

'Oh, come on,' he said, and what he meant was an invitation, a strain of consolation, but what came out was *disengaged. Fed up.* Knowing this in the turgid moment after he spoke, he still stood waiting, waiting for some sign of surrender or contrition from Alice that never came. Instead, she opened the cupboard, her narrow, off-white-sweatered back to him, and fetched down a bag of penne. Then she screamed and pulled the package taut before raising her arms and bringing it down swiftly, smashing the bag onto the pale green spackled tiles. The noodles spun out crazily, purposefully, like meteorites, like the beginnings of the world. Alice set her foot down – crunch! – on one small ridged tube before she began to sob.

Which was when Oldrick again did what he should not have. He smiled. The line between angry and absurd is a perforated one, but to cross that line is treacherous, especially where love is involved.

On Thursday, Oldrick's mother called.

'Dobre. We got a cheap flight to the old country, my sweet. We'll be gone two weeks. Two weeks with your poor old grandmamma before she dies.'

'Give her my love, Ma.'

'I will give it. Now, you know my will? My will is in the concertina file under the telephone table.'

'I know, Ma.'

'You know the concertina file? It's the one that looks like a babushka accordion. Under W for Will you will find it.'

'I know, Ma. Bon voyage.'

'Don't get intellectual with me. And hook up your air conditioner again, will you? Jesus help us, you are always a worry to me.'

Oldrick was trying to mix the colour of the raspberry coulis when he noticed it. It was a noise not unlike the sound of his own brain's blood if he pressed hard with his thumbs on his ears. It had ebbed that far inside. And it was coming from downstairs. When he reached the landing, he could smell sudsy earth-friendly floor cleaner. *Dah-oh, dah-oh*, went the sound. *Dah-oh, dah-oh*, behind his solar plexus now. There was a vent padded with white corrugated cardboard at the bottom of the stairs. He crouched near the vent and the sound was him.

Outside, the noise dissipated, although it seemed to have left some kind of residue on his insides. He swallowed to clear his ears. Through the front window of the café he could see the coffee guy dancing. Oldrick waved at him and mimed a sore head. 'Sore head,' he said to himself, and cradled his own head sympathetically. The coffee guy's gaze skimmed over Oldrick as if he were something inanimate, if slightly unusual – a recycling bin placed in the middle of the sidewalk on the wrong pickup day perhaps. Then he began to unroll the brindle-coloured utility mat that led to the door. He did this slowly, deliberately, flicking at the mat with the backs of his hands as if bidding it a snobbish farewell. When he reached the door he stopped, glanced again at Oldrick, then lifted up a sugar dispenser on a nearby table before dabbing underneath it with a yellow cloth he pulled from his back pocket.

The coffee guy, Oldrick gathered, was ignoring him. But Oldrick would wait. He would stand in his flip-flops, cut-offs and twelve-year-old Heineken T-shirt and wait. The coffee guy could not ignore him forever. It was hot and smelly and funny, Oldrick thought. To wait the way he was. It made him want to laugh out loud, to give off a true guffaw. He opened his eyes and mouth and tried it. Oldrick began to laugh. In order to laugh he had to take deeper breaths, which allowed the outside smell an access he had not thought possible, but also loosened his lungs and throat pleasantly.

At first the coffee guy, whose back was turned, did not seem to notice, but then something changed. While Oldrick laughed he stopped fiddling with the cappuccino machine and began, somehow, fiddling with himself. His hands were dug deep into the pockets of his black jeans, and at first Oldrick thought he must be reaching for a weapon, because of his gunslinger's stance. In that moment a great flare of indignant fear rose up in him. *It was not fair.* Him, Oldrick. Here, in Toronto. Outside a fair-trade coffee shop. *It was not fair.*

But it was not a gun at all. It was the coffee guy's penis. He had turned around and was standing, hands on hips, facing Oldrick through the glass, and though his face was swollen and red with rage, his exposed member remained limp and anemic, hanging out of his fly almost wistfully. He strode forward over the utility mat and resumed his stance less than a metre away from Oldrick, in front of the door. Then he began to yell, and as he yelled, he rolled his hips back and forth slightly, so that his pale, unseemly penis also rolled from side to side over the black denim of his jeans.

'How do you like that, eh, pal? Who's laughing now?'

Oldrick backed up a step and lost one of his flip-flops.

'Get your laughing gear around that, why don't you?' The coffee guy had now crouched down and was yelling through the crack under the Human Bean's door.

Oldrick opened the door to his apartment, stepped inside, locked the door and went upstairs to bed, where he did not sleep.

No one would believe it. He could not tell anyone. He would not tell anybody.

He told Steeney.

'People are a kind of changeable animal, Olds. They're unpredictable.' Her tone was magnanimous.

'It's sexual harassment, really.'

'Well, not exactly.'

'Whoa, are you saying I provoked it?'

'Chill, sister. Garden-variety lewdness is what it is.'

'Lewdness? Does that even still exist? It sounds like something from *Oliver Twist*.'

'You know, sometimes I have these fantasies about penises. Well, not exactly about penises, more about the thrusting action. But what's strange is that they aren't at all sexual – it's more connected to that ancient primal motion, I think, because whenever it happens it's as if I see this giant cock through, well, mist, almost, but then the mist is more like a thin layer of skin I have to peel back to see whose cock is thrusting, and when I get through all these "membranes" it's obvious the cock-bearer's identity is not important after all, since it's a sort of generic big-bodied guy with dark wavy hair.'

'That's *generic*? Does he have a beard?'

'Yes. And no. But sometimes stubble. There's something very Harlequin slash Professor of Socio-Political Theory about him.'

'I have a headache. I think it's because you keep saying *cock*.'

'Ninety percent of headaches are caused by dehydration.'

He called Lynn.

'Remember when you were talking about having a genuine grievance and an unreceptive audience? I mean, I know you were talking about, like, economic disparity and dire circumstance and everything, but … '

'Oh, Olds. I heard about Alice and that guy with the belt. What was his name again?'

'James,' he said. 'Thanks.'

'Something else?'

'Nope.'

He waited until he had hung up to cry.

That night, Saturday night, Oldrick sat on the steps inside his front door that led up to his apartment and, once again, he waited. When he was fourteen he had touched a corpse in a coffin. The corpse was his uncle, a drunk driver. When Oldrick reached out to touch his uncle's hand it felt like plasticine, with none of the fluid give and resistance of flesh. He had come to associate that plasticine feeling with not only death but recklessness, too – the alcohol having somehow given the man an unreal solidity and invincibility. Oldrick felt this invincibility now. It had been years since he had experienced this same raw anger, since the days – those Darwinian days – of the fourth grade, when Tommy Blatchford and Chris Sturino had tailed him around the perimeter of the yard, flanked him, then linked their arms through his, so they seemed a friendly trio sharing boy-gangster schemes. As they walked, Tommy and Chris would take turns blowing gently into his ears or onto his cheeks. *Phoo, phoo.* Then one or both of them would hiss: *Lazy Loafer.* Over and over again, *Lazy Loafer.* As they passed the piss zone near the library stairs: *Lazy Loafer.* As they skirted the baseball diamond, scuffing at the chalky gravel: *Lazy Loafer.* As they hurried by Melanie Rowlands with her flipped-up hair and lecherous limbs: *Lazy Loafer.* Oldrick did not know how to fight, but on day number seventeen, he learned. *I socked him*, he remembered thinking, as Tommy fell in a slow-motion diagonal onto the pavement. And socking was what it felt like, his fist entering the soft bit below his friend's ribcage (because they *were* friends, of that there was never any doubt). For a moment he even believed that the way his hand fit, he could actually have paraded around like that, with Tommy hoisted up triumphantly. Like a sock puppet.

But then Tommy hadn't moved. And then Tommy had, but barely. His feet pointed themselves of their own accord and quivered absurdly, while the rest of him stayed still and silent for long seconds. A gasp, and there – *there!* – was Tommy again, breathing, frantic for first aid and mothering. Oldrick had been suspended from school for two days, but not for one minute had he felt the weight or intention of his punishment.

The air in the stairwell was close and smelled overly sweet. For a moment Oldrick could not breathe. He put his head down between his knees and concentrated on the intake of oxygen, the one-two rhythm that was said to be instinctual. His hands were throbbing and sore, peeling in sixteen different places. In another, earlier, August, a bee got trapped in Ravi's armpit. It stung the skin of that tender underside three times before he could shake it free. Then it dropped, stunned, to the pavement at his feet. Ravi gave a gentle nod of recognition and sidestepped the bee respectfully as his skin began to swell and blister. He turned to Oldrick, pained, histamines a-flutter, and motioned to the bee. 'Poor thing, stuck under there. It's just in its nature to lash out, isn't it?'

Where did all the coffee guy's hate spring from? What childhood bog of battery and bad manners? Or was this lashing out simply, unapologetically, his *nature*? And if Oldrick could find out, follow bad deeds back like bread crumbs, would he even care what he discovered? The fact of the matter was that the coffee guy was just plain rude, and he had to be told. In the name of decency and community development, of which the cretin was supposed to be a champion!

Oldrick Pietraszek waited, smug with civilization.

At 11:49 p.m., when the coffee guy finally finished his chores and unlocked the front door of the Human Bean, Oldrick should have been there to greet him. And he was, although not as smoothly as he would have liked, nor as spry. The coffee guy had just stepped onto the sidewalk when Oldrick emerged, slowed by the heat but armed to the teeth with righteousness.

'Listen,' Oldrick said, and the coffee guy actually stopped and turned around. 'Can't we just talk to each other like human beings instead of making faces at each other through the glass?'

'I don't think so,' said the coffee guy, and began to walk away, just like that.

Oldrick could not say that he had at any other moment in his life been *gripped* by a sensation. But at that moment the desire to do physical harm to the coffee guy, to kick and kick at his shins, his head and his gut, had him in its sure vise.

'Wait!' Oldrick shouted. 'Come back here!' But he did not wait for the coffee guy to come back. He ran up and grabbed onto his arm, then spun him around so that the two men stood facing each other. The coffee guy stumbled slightly, regained his footing, then watched as Oldrick raised his fist. Oldrick stared into the coffee guy's eyes and felt frustration flashing like a strobe in his extremities.

'C'mon,' said the guy, and feigned a left hook.

But when Oldrick looked into his eyes again, he saw something he had not before. There was anger, yes, but also a swirling sad derision, something flapping then hurtling, desperate for a place to land. Oldrick lowered his fist without noticing, and the coffee guy understood the gesture for what it was: a foundering.

He sniffed at Oldrick, then spoke. 'Screw you, scumbag,' said the coffee guy, and turned on his heel neatly, like a jazz dancer.

When Oldrick looked out his window from upstairs, he could still see him retreating into the city night in his slouchy sleeveless shirt, doing a blasé sashay down the deserted lamplit street. It was then that Oldrick wished, pointlessly, and with all of his soul, that he had seen the last of him.

The next morning – a Sunday! – the garbage trucks came back, clanking and helpful. The garbage on the street disappeared into the compactors, and the trucks drove off, with the collectors clinging on like carbuncles, then vanished. They may have been motoring north then west to a place designated for waste, a pit ringed with toxins and overly brave black bears. Or south, across the border, to be deposited in someone else's backyard. In any case, other people's garbage remained a matter of chance and circumstance, politics and protest songs. And on that particular Sunday morning, Oldrick decided there was not much he could do to change any one of these slippery constants. He turned off his phone, bought a fan, donned some surgical gloves, mixed a new coulis colour and began his series of well-endowed miniature buffalo (five by seven inches, oil on canvas), which was one day to end up in a foyer display of the home of Eileen Thibaud, a corpulent, sensual and swift-talking Montreal art collector of above-average intelligence, limited fame and impeccable taste.

NOT QUITE CASABLANCA

1 JESUS' FEET

'You like museums and architecture, I hope. This place is *all* about the culture.'

Lisa nodded. *All about the culture?* Why was her aunt talking like a sitcom? Carla was supposed to be the one solid element of this whole set-up, and instead she was acting wacky, like an old aunt. Which she wasn't. Which Lisa did not want her to be. Maybe it was not a good idea for her to be here. On the plane to Madrid she felt cosmopolitan, well-read, although this was her first trip to Europe and the book in her bag was something Vince had loaned her that looked and felt much too heavy, in more ways than one. She ate everything they put in front of her, compartment by compartment, slid her feet out of her shoes and watched the movie obediently. A beautiful woman was playing a cop who was playing a beauty queen. Long legs and hijinks. She liked it. To be in the sky, though, that was amazing. The clouds were the texture of cheese, or sugary rock strata, so eminently touchable it could not be true they were atmosphere only. Then – land! – the clouds' muddy counterparts, slapped down like cow patties on the sea.

'We'll just take a short walking tour through the city, then check out the Prado. I think you'll be blown away. Only a day, though, it's not a lot of time.' Her aunt was beetling around the small room of their pension, tugging at the bedspread, gathering small shiny gift-wrapped soaps and tossing them into her purse. She stopped when she noticed Lisa watching her. 'Sorry, force of habit.'

Lisa was tired. She could hear mopeds outside making the same messy raspberry sounds she made with Luke, the three-year-old she babysat back home. Amplified. When the gauzy beige curtain blew back from the window she could see that outside was a carnival. It was a carnival of Spaniards doing their Spanish thing in the hot Spanish sun. There was a digital clock kitty-corner to the pension, but she could not quite make out the time. Definitely too early. She walked over to the window, opened it and peered out, but the clock was no longer showing the time. Instead the rectangular red numbers read forty-two. It was forty-two degrees at, at … a really early time in the morning.

'They make strong coffee in this country, don't they?'

Her aunt nodded and looped a cardigan through her purse strap.

'I don't think you'll need a sweater today.'

'No.' But the cardigan stayed looped.

They went for espressos in the downstairs café where objects, faces, began to gain integrity, logic, some inherent speediness.

Madrid's airport had ceilings so high you could almost, but not quite, believe you were outside, multilingual pronouncements that babbled from above and an incredible array of perfume and booze in bottles that looked almost, but not quite, the same. Foreign, but fine. It was not until Lisa had pulled her bag like a dead body into the appointed café that something began to splinter. While she was waiting for her aunt she had ordered a *sandwich vegetal*, which was not a vegetable sandwich at all but two mayonnaise-slathered pieces of fried bread with a fried egg between, a pale pink tomato slice on the side. And what had stupefied her, more than the bright new ochre landscapes, the swarthy men at the counter downing shots of thick espresso, was the egg yolk. It was orange, the reddish orange of a sunset. It seemed to her to indicate something bloody and unholy about the chicken itself. Some leakage in the intestine or bladder, one of those spongy dun-coloured elimination organs. How could this be? Should she tell someone? She didn't tell anyone. She couldn't remember the word for *disgusting* in Spanish. Not *vegetal* obviously.

The museum was colossal and quiet, like something God had built then abandoned. Not that quiet, with the people. Tourists chasing down culture. Lisa was one of them, and it smarted a little. She whizzed through the rooms, happy for the air conditioning and smooth gleaming floors, and ended up at the gift shop, which was better. She loved the postcard reproductions of the paintings, the stacks of them. In front of the paintings themselves she wilted a little. Where was a person supposed to put her hands while watching great art? She bought six postcards of paintings she remembered, the famous ones, pocketed them and went to meet her aunt in the cafeteria.

Over tapas, which was Spanish snacks, Aunt Carla began to talk.

'Did you see that painting, *La Coronación de espinas* by Anton Van Dyck? My God, it sent me into some strange orbit. Jesus is sitting there about to be crucified, and all around him is commotion and accusation. They've very thoughtfully tucked his hair behind his ears, and they're lowering this thorny crown onto his head. And all the while he looks so ... reconciled. His eyes are kind of half-closed, like he has a bad head cold and he just wants someone to bring him a bowl of hot soup. His feet. Jesus, his feet. Such long toes reaching down – like rain! The space between the big toe and the rest, clumped together – almost a cloven hoof, really, isn't it? That had to have been deliberate. The way they're clinging so fiercely to the ground, like claws, or the tines of a fork sunk into soil ...'

'I didn't notice that one.' Lisa had, but she preferred the Goya with the drowning dog. Jesus was overdone. At home they were converting all the churches into condos, and she wasn't fazed. She hoped her aunt hadn't gotten all into God these last few years.

Carla rubbed her arms briskly, but not because she was cold. God almighty. Jesus' feet. She'd done it this time. She'd noticed it, this tendency to blurt like a convert. It was natural, she supposed. The closer we are to death, our own or someone else's, the more likely we are to speak in aphorisms, unashamedly, baldly, without self-consciousness. It is not only that we believe these otherwise slightly embarrassing statements to be true, but that we feel confident, even bold and confrontational articulating them. Still, poor Lisa. She would buy her a sundress or something.

2 WITHOUT PEOPLE LIKE THEM

When they touched down in Gran Canaria, the *calima* had already wafted in. A thick mustard-coloured haze hung above and throughout Las Palmas, grainy smog made solid that caught in your lungs.

'It's the sands of the Sahara, blown over from Africa,' Lisa's aunt told her in the cab into Triana. 'You can divide the world up into jigsaw pieces, but nothing will ever stay in one place. It all gets mixed up in the end. For better or worse. Do up your seat belt.'

Lisa nodded and clicked the metal tongue into place over her left hip. She was badly dressed for the weather, the place. Her khaki shorts and strappy flat sandals felt safari-like, sturdy. Through the window she could see the women here matched the brightly coloured buildings; they wore pastels made intense, well-fitted skirts, spindly heels. She was conscious of a certain horsiness to her appearance that had nothing to do with her clothes. Although a city girl, she had been taught to take up space, enjoy her food, go treading quietly through the woods on weekends – unless in bear country, in which case it was a good idea to tramp purposefully and ring a cowbell. She was workmanlike as a person, and she had never noticed it before.

Her aunt nudged her. 'We're closer here to Africa than Spain, you know.'

Lisa had an accordioned map in her knapsack, the edges pale and soft from folding and refolding. 'I know. Almost Casablanca.'

'Not quite Casablanca. Not quite.'

It could be it was not a good thing for Lisa to be here, Carla thought. Not quite Spain. Not quite Africa. *I'm not quite myself*, she whispered, in her best Ingrid Bergman. Six weeks of this. The cab was nearing the flat she had rented; she recognized the wind of the streets, the *tienda* on the corner, the frog fountain. Their apartment was a block away from the cathedral, next to the museum. Carla acknowledged this as an ironic choice, and was pleased with herself to the point that the decision ceased to be about irony and was instead tinged by an uncomplicated pathos. They'd share a wall with the room where they stored the skulls of the aboriginals, the Guanche, who had perished valiantly with the spread of the colonists. On one of these streets was a statue of a Guanche warrior falling headfirst off a cliff, his body ropy with muscle. They had preferred it, this reckless airborne cartwheel, to any of the entertainments the Spaniards had to offer. She would have to show Lisa that; it was unbelievable and darkly thrilling. Did she believe that having Lisa here would ease her own fall somehow? It was superstitious and selfish to think so, to lure her across the ocean for the purposes of distraction only. There was more to it.

'It's so strange and hazy out there,' she said to Lisa, who nodded.

'Is it like this all the time in the desert?' Lisa tapped on the glass, as if testing it.

It was a question, but she didn't seem to expect an answer, which was good since Carla had none. The last time she was home she had gone to see a 3-D movie about the disappearing rainforest. Everyone wore ridiculous pink cardboard wraparound glasses and stared, rapt, at the screen. At one point she found herself reaching out to touch a quivering dew-covered leaf, only to find nothing. It was like a mirage. It *was* a mirage.

'Do you think we might be able to visit Casablanca?'

Carla sensed it was another non-question, but she answered anyway. 'Nope. Too far. Too expensive.'

Vince thought Ingrid Bergman was stunning because of her eyebrows. 'Every time she's thinking or remembering, you can see it in those brows. It's incredible. It's what the movie is all about.'

Vince was from New York.

'Not quite New York. Yonkers, actually.'

'Isn't it the same thing?'

'Not really.'

Lisa liked Vince because he was sarcastic, slightly chubby and never wore V-necks. She told him this when they were flirting and brave. Vince liked her, she suspected, because of the way she pronounced her vowels. They had met in the courtyard of her Toronto high school, Lakeside Collegiate, in late March. Lisa was helping Mee-Yung smoke a cigarette; Mee-Yung was helping Lisa to understand.

'No, they actually snip something under the baby's tongue to improve their pronunciation.'

'Improve their pronunciation of what? They're babies, for Chrissakes. They don't *pronounce* anything yet.'

'But these people are rich, fuck. They just want their kids to be the best businessmen, and that means speaking the best English.'

'You speak English.' Lisa took a puff of the cigarette, but carefully. She still wasn't a regular.

'Yeah, but I'm gifted. The Queen of Tongues.' Mee-Yung waggled her tongue at Lisa and grabbed back the cigarette.

'Gifted, yeah.'

'You better write me when you're doing your big tour of Europe, missy.'

Then Mee-Yung was gone from the bench, the back of her head sleek down the street, her empty knapsack slung on one sloping shoulder. And just as suddenly Vince was there.

Lisa could tell he was about to introduce himself. 'My parents don't really like Americans,' she said.

'Why?'

'Uh, you take our water, give us your dirty air, send our jobs to Mexico, you're really nice but you're also kind of rude and you don't really know we exist.'

He gave her a look. It was a look that was wounded, surprised and sly at once.

'We can't stop watching your TV shows.'

'But you're kind of dependent on us, aren't you?'

She winced.

He stared into her eyes, which was unnerving in the same way sushi for the first time is unnerving. Something so close to being alive just sitting there in your mouth.

Lisa looked up and out through the window. They drove past a cathedral with a wedding party waiting outside. The sun was shining strong on the faces of the men, who wiped sweat from their chins and concentrated harder on the women's smooth, sinewed calves. The cab was slowing and now stopping.

'We're here.'

The door to their apartment was very tall. Like a door for a Spanish giant, or possibly a pirate. What would happen if she just refused to go inside? Could she live on the beach? Would the *calima* cover her when she wasn't looking? *I'll be a dune.*

Lisa wasn't getting out of the cab. Maybe she didn't like the look of the place. To Carla, it looked good. To Carla it looked like the closest thing to home. But not without Lisa; she'd had enough of alone time. She'd made it sound to her brother as if she had come into extra cash, suddenly, for a reason that had to do with rebates or bonuses. Some quirky European boon. But there were details she thought it best he didn't know. In his last e-mail: *Don't go filling Lisa's head with any of your philosophies. That's the last thing we need – a teenage daughter on some kind of quest!* To show he was friendly, half-joking, Robert had included a sideways smiley made of punctuation marks. This was the problem. They wanted to punctuate everything with a smile, when she would much prefer a shout. And what teenager, no matter how boxed up in her family and feelings, was not on a quest?

Lisa poked Carla in the ribs, friendly-like.

Had she said that last part out loud?

'Do you have the key for these monsters?' A wave towards the double doors.

'Mmm. In my purse somewhere.' She fished out the key, inserted and turned it resolutely, and they were inside.

They dragged the bags up thirty-eight stairs.

'We'll need to buy a few things. It's not completely furnished. A soft chair or two maybe.'

'Okay,' said Lisa, '*okay*.' A soft chair was something.

Carla watched her niece trail from room to room. She'd always seen something in Lisa, a glimmer of herself, or something perhaps more expansive, farther-reaching, that she could not glimpse in her brother, Robert, and his wife, Cynthia, in their stolid red-brick Toronto house. Their ways, their quaint, for-show arguments about how to open a boiled egg. The tip-tapping followed by the scoop with the tiny spoon? Or the quick, decisive slice with a knife? All the earnest striving for good and decency. She could appreciate it in a remote sort of way; she saw its worth and applauded it politely. *Where would we be without people like them?* But why hadn't they *moved*? To Cuba once, it's true, to really get a sense of the culture, they said, to understand better the sharing way of life. But nowhere else, except on vacation. Canada's coasts – Newfoundland's craggy beauty, Nova Scotia's bit of Britain. Salty, rough-hewn places. Then Vancouver, where everywhere you looked was like a giant, peopled postcard. She suspected they felt somehow superior in their rootedness, but how could you feel it, really feel it – life's edges, life's edginess – in one place, and in Canada, for God's sake? No, you had to force yourself to *move*.

'The bathroom's completely huge! I could practically sleep in there.' Lisa poked her pointed pale face into the living room, where Carla was reclining, sort of, in a bamboo bucket chair. 'Should we unpack?'

'Nah, let's have a drink first. I'll grab some vino from the store. You relax.'

Lisa heard them, the thirty-eight steps, as they slapped up against Carla's clogs, then the giant doors, a gasp of street traffic, and silence, self. 'Hello, self,' she said. 'You're in Spain. Las Canarias.' She walked into the palatial bathroom and stood on the bidet so that she could see her whole reflection in the makeup mirror. '*Mamá mia*,' she whispered, and stuck out her hip. '*Ay caramba!*' She hadn't wanted to come on the trip originally, but then her father made a runty, rueful face and said *it probably wasn't such a good idea anyway* and she cottoned on. Her mother had shrugged, resigned, it seemed, and blown her breath upwards into her blonde fringe. Cynthia loved Toronto because it was so multi-cultural. There was no need to travel abroad, really, in such a city. She liked to collect newly arrived strays, have them round for dinner. She and Robert vivaciously tasted and pointedly swallowed the food their guests offered in large steaming pans or fragrant, foil-covered bowls. It was implied in Lisa's family that people from other countries who *had endured hardship* were somehow more virtuous, perhaps less prone to petty cruelty than those who *had been born into relative privilege*. It could be this was true. In any case, it made Lisa alternately apologetic and lazy when it came to politics and travel. She knew how lucky she was, from dinner-table conversation and from compulsive, eloquent cab drivers – Ethiopian, Croatian, Afghani. They had stories. They had been lucky; they were safe now. Lucky and safe, said Lisa's mother's gaze, a message confirmed, given voice by her father's stance. Vince's parents were not together.

'My dad's some hot-shit-in-a-wineglass business guy in Manhattan. I don't really see him. Very much.'

'Too bad.'

'Yeah. I tried them once, you know.'

'What?'

'V-necks.'

'Too bad.'

'Yeah.'

3 PATA NEGRA

In the mornings, her aunt made *cortados*, sweet and milky coffee, and they sat on the balcony, listening to the bells of the cathedrals. Or they walked the streets, dodging the compact cars, which somehow seemed more dangerous and clever than the slick, tall-tired Jeeps of home. The shopping district was stressful and wonderful, with its stores packed with pants that actually fit and impossibly poised saleswomen. Near the bus depot was a square where they often stopped to eat almond biscuits and watch the passersby.

In the northwest corner of the square, three African women lounged standing up. On the interlocking stone in front of them, they had placed a large sarong patterned with purple and mustard-coloured moons and stars. On top of this were scattered wooden carvings of giraffes and gazelles, twiggy legs and elegant necks, all shellacked to a hard shine. Lisa was studying the face of the woman nearest her when a lithe man in complicated sports sandals stopped, fingered a small chunky elephant, frowned and replaced it clumsily on its side so that its thick stiff legs rested parallel to the sarong's moons and stars. The vendor's face was broad, with cheekbones that appeared to be straining away from each other, and when her nostrils flared, Lisa got the impression of something overstuffed and volatile. Her aunt had noticed her watching the vendors.

'Most Canarians don't want them here. The Africans.'

'Why?' Lisa said, although she didn't really want to know, with bits of buttery biscuit still on her tongue, a child trundling by, waving at her as though she were important.

'Well, they're lazy, aren't they? Don't really like to work when push comes to shove.'

When push comes to shove. Her aunt was testing or taunting her, or both. She had been here before, with Mee-Yung, and probably with others.

They sat at the high, hard benches in the Biology room, in pairs, like the animals in Noah's ark, whispering in solidarity over their Bunsen burners. The teacher was balding and thin, with tiny blotchy hands he flung about in explanation, talking shop: sheep and copies of sheep, more sheep, then hearts, and more hearts, copies of copies. Science could be that dogged and that magical.

'Look at her hair,' hissed Mee-Yung, and jerked her head towards the new Chinese student who was broad-shouldered, her face fierce and sure. She seemed athletic under her tight-fitting flared jeans, confident. 'Maybe she washed it, like, last month. That's just like the Chinese.'

Lisa was surprised at Mee-Yung's vehemence. Mee-Yung and the Chinese girl looked the same, she thought, and she meant they must *be* the same. But they weren't. Korea and China were very different places. As different as ... Italy and Iqaluit. You should never hate someone because they looked different from you. And you should never assume people who seemed the same were in cahoots. No one type of human had a patent on hate. Still, it was unfair what Mee-Yung was saying, wasn't it?

'They're just dirty. They don't believe in showers and they like to hork and spit all over the place.'

'Really?'

'Totally. It's a superstition. They think if they take too many showers it will steal their spirits or something.' Mee-Yung pushed one of her bangles authoritatively up her arm.

'You mean they think the water is bewitched or cursed?' The question came out gleeful. Why? It had something to do with Mee-Yung's dismissive certainty; she wanted to believe her. She wanted to feel that sure, to marshal evidence.

'Mmm. Some complete craziness.' Mee-Yung pulled a palm pilot from under the desk. 'Let's send her a message.'

'You don't have her address, do you?'

'Can't be too hard. Dirtychink@chopsuey.com. Or something along those lines.'

'Mee!'

'Joking, jeez.' Mee-Yung did a drum roll on her notebook with her pen, and seemed prepared to absorb herself in the experiment being demonstrated up front.

There was a slide projected on the wall: something fleshy and exposed.

'What about the spitting?'

'What?'

'Why do they spit?'

'Oh. I dunno. Too much phlegm, I guess.' Mee-Yung slid the palm pilot back into her pocket and faked a yawn so that she could stretch her arm around Lisa's shoulders. 'Don't trouble yourself, my friend. We got da pow-ah.'

Then the bell rang loudly, and it was time to get up and move along.

Back on the bench, Carla's eyebrows were arched severely. What was she trying to pull? Lisa got up and began walking towards the sarong. She would right the elephant, put it back on its feet. It seemed important to her that she do this. But when she got close, she found she could not; the vendors would believe she wanted to buy, or that she was mocking them. She turned back towards her aunt, who was still sitting, hands placed firmly, palms down, on the bench to either side of her, as if she were bracing herself for something.

On the city beach, Las Canteras, everyone was out. Whole families lolled and took turns smearing each other's backs with coconut-smelling lotion. Kids gambolled in the surf while old women and men sat with their breasts, bums and bellies sagging towards the sand. Lisa and Carla paid 500 pesetas each for their white slatted beach chairs, then an extra 300 for the umbrella. You had to buy shade in Las Palmas. A man walked by, chanting. *Hay Coca-Cola, hay Fanta, hay Tropical.* Carla waved him over, then asked Lisa to decide. They ended up with two Tropicals. Pale, fizzed-up, barely there beer.

'I thought it would be juice.'

'Nah-ah. Beer. If they run out they'll serve you Dorada. It's the beer of Tenerife. There's a rivalry.'

Sometimes living on an island was a bit high-school. Lisa took a swig and worked the can into the sand just under her chair to prevent spillage. Carla adjusted the back of her chair so she could see the water and the people.

'When I was a kid there was this variety store at the corner of Lansdowne and Bloor. More like a newsagent's, really, but they had this kind of glorified cooler at the back. They were Portuguese, the owners.' Carla couldn't tell if Lisa was listening. Her eyes were closed.

'Every day I went in there and bought a pop. Or not, if I didn't have the money, but I'd still go in to see.'

Lisa opened one eye and brought a hand up to block the sun. 'To see what?'

'The selection.'

'Oh.' She closed her eyes again.

'Because I had a system then, or more like an orderly kind of superstition, where I believed each drink could help me in a different way, depending on how I was feeling at the time.' But Carla knew that it had been faith, more than superstition. Children are not superstitious. It seemed to her that at some level, in order to be superstitious you actually had to suspect your belief was somehow faulty, something that belonged in storybooks or the sixteenth century, yet still persist, stubbornly, in believing it. Children did not choose to believe these things, they simply wove them completely, unquestioningly, into their everyday.

'Magic medicine,' Lisa said to the sky.

'Sort of, but I'm not sure I believed it was the pop or juice exactly whose ingredients were transformative. It was more like the drink's, I dunno, aura or something.'

'Mmm.'

'Cuckoo, eh?'

'Mmm. So why didn't you choose the drink from *el hombre*?' She waved her hand towards the cold-drinks man, whose red cooler was still visible a few hundred metres down the beach.

'Dunno. Not sure how I want to feel?'

'Mmm. Open your beer, Carla.'

'Okay.' Carla let Lisa believe she had *mmm*ed her way to the upper hand. She knew teenaged cynicism, and liked it. It was a relief to tell that story. She remembered the small shopkeeper's tightly wound denim apron, his swath of shining black hair and snub nose, his air of comforting indifference. *Obrigado*, she used to say, as the heavy clanging door swung shut behind her and the condensation from the bottle moistened her palm.

'I'm going for a swim.' Lisa swung her legs to one side of her chair and fiddled pointlessly with the tie at the neck of her swimsuit.

'Okay – ' Okay, be careful. Okay, have fun. Okay, be safe. Which one should she choose? She remembered the day Lisa was born, the hard look in her brother's eyes. He would not let her down; he and Cynthia would not allow her to fall – she would be suspended, well-shod feet dangling above the viscera of this earth, until they deemed her ready. An aunt, a godfather, a grandparent do not have these propensities for protection; they are instead lavish, unrestricted in the gifts they grant their exceptional little ones. She wanted – no, *willed* – Lisa to know hard, satisfying work (cattle ranching?), all manners of whimsy, Japanese and the electric guitar. She wanted her to have everything.

The sun was lower in the sky, but more focused, hotter than it had been at noon. Carla pulled her bag from under her chair and handed Lisa a baguette and a bottle of water, which Lisa placed on the towel under her chair.

'Not hungry?'

'Not quite. Do you have a boyfriend?'

'Not at the moment. Not for some moments, actually. Why? Do you?'

'Not quite. Not exactly. We're just hanging out.'

'Ah. What's his name?'

'Vince.'

'Vince or Vincent?'

'Vincent's too vampire-slash-missing-ear. Vince is better.'

'Okay, Vince.' Carla noticed Lisa was blushing. She must have been quoting him.

'So, what's his story?'

'He's pretty cool. Moved to Toronto with his mom for a year, maybe longer. From New York. Into film.'

'New York, eh?' Why did men always make women slightly stupid? She could see Lisa had fallen hard for this Vince. Any advice she might toss out to her would be deliberately overlooked. Carla still netted them sometimes, men's stares, and she could play them out, if she was inclined. Mostly, she was not inclined. She knew she was not beautiful. She was slim but boxy – a friendly face with features slightly too pronounced, as if they'd been traced with charcoal pencil for effect. A man had once told her that it was the intelligence that puckered around her mouth that had drawn him to her, but Carla was not sure this same intelligence would not be mistaken for a scattered shrewishness in a different light, with more conservative earrings. While their mother was alive, and she and Robert were still corresponding regularly, they had joked about the way her mother assessed her: *Doesn't look good on paper. Twice divorced. Teacher, baker, candlestick maker. Flighty.*

Not well, they could now add, as her mother had been euphemistically inclined.

'Who do you prefer, Humphrey or the other guy, Paul something?'

'Ah, Humphrey, I guess, but it's just all so black and white.'

'That's its charm, Carla.'

'Right.' But *Casablanca* made Carla angry. It hadn't always, with its intrigue, fedoras and piano tunes. Now it made her feel deceived. All storybook, and decisions less wrenching than they should have been, really. The way they play-acted at importance and infidelities. All of those edge-of-war heroics. She couldn't bear it; it was too easy. And for some reason the word itself, or maybe the entire concept – *Casablanca* – had come to be associated with another foreign-sounding word in her brain: *chemotherapy*.

She shook off her irritation, stuck her hand back in her beach bag and struck gold.

'What you got there?' Lisa was hungry now.

'It's Pata Negra. An incredible delicacy. They feed the pig only black acorns its whole life to fatten it up. Try it.'

'I'm pretty much a vegetarian.'

'What do you mean?' And why hadn't Carla noticed before?

'I still eat fish, because fish are ugly and prehistoric with those small beady eyes, and I kind of think they deserve it. Cute lambs, no. Fish, *no problema*.' Lisa hesitated, noticed her tummy and attempted a tuck. 'Besides, *Pata Negra*? It sounds racist.'

'Don't be ridiculous. Eat some of this. If you really want to save the planet and beat the evil corporations, you should go to the London School of Economics and learn to fight them on their own level. You'll never get another chance to try this. The world can wait.'

'Nope.'

'You little shit. I kind of like you.' Carla cuffed her niece across the head like they were hockey players on the same team. She considered her towel. A twirl and flick.

'I know.'

'What?'

'I know you like me.'

'Right. Get my back, will you? I'm starting to burn.'

4 WHAT LISA KNEW

On the way to Puerto de las Nieves, the crumbling mountains near the highway wore giant hairnets to keep them from falling onto the road. Lisa was getting used to it now: the bougainvillea, the prickly pear cacti, the tall feather-duster palm trees, the tough oversized thistles that bordered the paths. All the buildings so old and *historical*. None of this seemed odd anymore. Instead, her mind kept tripping up over licence plates. There were millions of them, all particular, all different, all Spanish, zooming by that woman, over there, hanging that turquoise T-shirt on a line, without comment or apparent thought. How did they get away with it? So many other bodies just living as if they *could*. It was almost too much for the mind to bear, licence plates and other people's laundry. Oh, but she was glad to be on a bus and away from Carla. She loved her, and as a roommate she was ideal, but she was her *aunt*. When Lisa was a child, Carla had contrived elaborate treasure hunts. Lisa and her friends crept around Carla's apartment searching for the squares of paper she had crumpled behind plant pots, rolled and perched on windowsills, tucked behind the toilet tank. The clues were strange snippets of the *who am I?* variety. *I live amongst the sweet and starved, I keep your pencils straight, up-wharved. Who am I? I* was a cylindrical glazed pot with pens and pencils and paintbrushes poking upwards from its opening like porcupine quills, wedged between a pile of old fashion magazines and a bowl of hard strawberry candies on an end table in Carla's bedroom.

'*Up-wharved* is not a proper word, Carla,' she had exclaimed, with the righteous indignation of the perfect speller. 'Who says,' had come the reply, 'who says?' And Lisa wasn't sure who had said, it just was. Which was something Carla didn't understand sometimes. Acceptance. Lisa had all of her old colouring books filed in her bookcase at home. The purple bears wearing South American headdresses were Carla's doing. Lisa could still see the tidy brown cross-hatching underneath that she had begun and had to abandon when her aunt took over. People and things (bears even) had their boundaries; to jump out of them was messy. When she was younger, more malleable and oblivious, she had not felt the weight of Carla's expectation, but now it hung in the air around her like the *calima*. She had jumped at the chance of this field trip on her own. She needed some time to pin some thoughts down, tidy them.

What she knew was that Carla was sick, probably dying. She knew this from the flights of philosophy, the stolen stares and, more concretely, the pill bottles that had clattered like a wild abacus in her aunt's makeup bag when she picked it up. A search in the local internet café had yielded several near-encyclopedic sites on non-Hodgkin's lymphoma. She read them over carefully, then wrote a long, broken-hearted e-mail to Vince, which she did not send. Carla had not told her, or anybody else, about the cancer, which meant, Lisa supposed, that she did not want her to know. Besides, what could she *know*, really? About dying, or renegade cells multiplying? And wasn't trying to know, *truly* know, a kind of *patronizing*? She knew what she knew only: her own now-tanned skin a sac for boisterous blood, and thoughts that could act as balm or blister depending on the circumstances. Depending on how she chose to direct them.

But then there were things Lisa had been trying *not* to know. Her aunt's delicate, fuzzed-up head, a small slick of vomit on the bathroom tiles. An African woman dancing angry on the streets, while a Guanche warrior tumbled, endlessly, into the night. Mee-Yung's dextrous, dangerous tongue. It all got mixed up together in the end.

Puerto de las Nieves was a cove surrounded by jutting black cliffs of finely perforated rock, a beach full of cigarette butts and surf like shaving cream. A fisherman in grey slacks and a thin belt with a blue bucket at his feet stood near the shore ignoring Lisa as she wiggled into her swimsuit under her dress, then crouched to pee. She found a spot to sit and tried to read Vince's novel, but it only made her think of Vince, his July-city smell when he had handed it to her. She wanted him there touching her. They had not had sex yet, which meant that she was too ugly or too Canadian. He was from New York. She imagined that meant plenty of gritty, skinny, high-strung options of the beauty queen/cop variety. Oh, but she wanted that love: his skin on hers. She sighed and decided to find a place to eat. Poor substitute, but.

She chose a restaurant and was ignored by the maître d'; a young woman alone, *sola*, didn't mean much, it seemed. She loitered by the door in her flip-flops, trying not to appear homeless. Then, finally seated, she got full on the tasty, textured soup and couldn't finish the fish. The maître d' whisked away her plates and took her money.

Back on the beach she began to think of herself like in an airport novel or a movie they might show on an airplane. *She arranged herself delicately on her buttery-yellow beach towel. The humidity caused the tendrils at the back of her neck to curl and sag. No sooner had she swept the sand off her thighs than she was interrupted by a gang of young men on mopeds.*

There were four of them, the boys on mopeds, ranging in age from fifteen, she guessed, to twenty-one. They roared up and dismounted like rock stars, stamping their feet and pumping their fists in the air. Then they laughed, a bit louder than they needed to, and two of them took off their shirts. Lisa found herself deliberately trying to appear confident, as they were, and the knowledge of this all-round sham made her both cross and amused. Here now were numbers five and six, skidding to a stop and slapping high-fives. One-upmanship all around. What was the competition? It didn't seem to matter, and Lisa could not decipher their banter, which was not the polite shopkeeper's Spanish she was used to, but instead a series of shouts and inflections of which she recognized only a few words: *Moto. Pescador. Mi mamá.* And the song, the words to the song, these also she thought she understood. They had been singing it since they arrived, passing it between them, so that for seconds at a time it would fade out, before it was picked up again, made strong by someone's not entirely tuneful enthusiasm. At the moment it was one of the younger boys who had adopted it. He stood in one spot and held his elbows high, clapping as he sang, watching the ocean, then glancing at each of his friends in turn, before turning to stare at Lisa with a borderline sexual smirk. Nevertheless, she felt included. *Ay, corazón,* came the chorus, and the boy beat at his tanned chest, which rose ridged and bony above his baggy yellow surfer shorts. *Ay, ay, corazón.*

'More like square dancers than Spaniards,' observed Lisa to her right knee, which, she noticed, was more rectangular and protruding than she would have liked. Then she wished Vince was around to hear her observation, and at the same time wished she was one of the boys doing the stamping, and at the same time observed a strange-shaped buoy on the ocean, bobbing spastically this way and that.

Carla was sitting at home on the balcony, not thinking of anything in particular, save maybe the distinct angle of the sun on the white-washed concrete of the wall and the way the building next to hers cut cleanly through the steeple at a diagonal, forming a slice of cathedral and sky, that could, if you let it, make you slightly dizzy. She had hung some of their laundry, hers and Lisa's, on the clothes tree. There were tank tops and underwear shining stiff in the sun.

She liked them there, had always found in the intermingling of clothes, dirty or clean, a sense of small but noteworthy intimacy. With lovers, usually. But this, too, with her niece. She walked over to a nearby pair of shorts, fingered them for dryness. Her neighbour across the way was waving at her. Why? Usually she leaned all the way out her window and spoke slurringly in a friendly, unmitigated sort of way, to which Carla smiled eagerly, understandingly, then retreated. They were both, she imagined, pleased with this, and she found the repetition of *sí, sí, sí*, doubly pleasing for the fact that neither of them really did seem to see at all. But now the neighbour seemed to be calling her over, deliberately, with the sense of ceremony people feel compelled to put on at serious occasions. Carla leaned over the wall of the balcony, and the woman held out her hands to her.

'*Americana, sí?*'

'*No, canadiense.*' Abroad, being Canadian was like being part of a second-tier sports team you never knew existed. There was a secret swelling pride to it.

'*Ah, canadiense. Hay una gran tragedia en Nueva York.*' The neighbour held her lips away from her teeth as she spoke, and Carla understood, not for the first time, what it was like to be kindly condescended to by a stranger.

'*Qué?*'

'*La televisión, señora. Mira la televisión.*' She shook her head impatiently.

Carla ran inside and grabbed a wrap – she would never have worn a wrap, dusty rose and fringed, in Canada – then ran down the thirty-eight steps, onto the narrow street and into a café, where there was a bustle of words made emphatic by Spanish and nascent panic. *Terrorista. Terrorista.* That open 'a' at the end, part discovery, part scream. She didn't like it. But where was the television? Finally, in the third bar she visited, there it was. A plane, a building, a fire, a tragic, uncalled-for crumple. Newscasters trying on serious faces for themselves. How does it feel? She should find Lisa, get Lisa and bring her home. She raced to the bus station and sat uncomfortably at the back of an air-conditioned coach, her blood pumping too hard and fast, really, for her to remain sedentary. Lisa had a friend in New York, didn't she? Were they lovers? Lisa would think that term too old-fashioned, or art-school. Too *Casablanca*.

She took a long stride from the step to the curb when the bus arrived, then ran past the tourist stalls and rowdy restaurants to the beach. The boardwalk felt strange under her feet, bouncy, and she realized, through her panicked resolution, how good it felt to run as if she meant it.

There was a Sunday, three years ago, when Carla was living in Mojácar, in a small flat she rented from a family of eight who called her Señora Canadiense (which made her think of long satin sashes, beauty pageants), when she joined in the Festival de San Isidro. She had been walking through the square outside the town's community centre when she saw a convoy of trucks decorated with streamers and the waxen figure of the saint, whose face and demeanour were suspiciously Jesus-like, although an effort had been made to differentiate him in dress. He wore the vines and flowers and symbols of plenty he was known for as the saint of the fields, and these, combined with the paper lanterns that surrounded him, made for an aura of carnivalesque piety and benevolence. A portly, gleamingly bald man had gestured to her to climb up. So she had, and the trucks had motored slowly through the town, down onto the plain to Turre, where they unloaded and there was free food for everybody: styrofoam plates of olives and crusty bread, hot pink meats bejewelled with fat, and small nubs of cheese. The wives danced together in straw hats and aerobic shoes to the eight-piece band, their tummies solidly protruding over their walking shorts. Carla had caught the eye of one of them, who held her gaze, then gave an exaggerated wink. She remembered the winking woman was wearing a flat-topped boater with a wide brim and an overlong T-shirt with *Boston* stencilled in swirling letters on the front. She was sipping Fanta Limón from a can. Then back on the trucks and to the beachside town of Garrucha, along the water, the band playing *oh-blah-dee*, the sun beating its dry way down, past the white towering domes of the hotels, the straining cranes and scaffolding, the bodies prone and oily on the beach, all the way to the end of the line, the band playing 'Yellow Submarine' and Frank Sinatra's 'My Way.' Up, up, into the mountains and the town of Sopalmo, where the men were swallowed by the town's sole bar and the women and children disappeared into the brush with picnic baskets and long sandwiches wrapped in tin foil, and when she asked the ice cream vendor where everyone had gone, he replied, *Fresa o chocolate?*

Sometimes, when she imagined it – the end – this is how she believed it might be: the truck through the fields, down to the sea and up through the mountains, the inevitability, the rush of wind, the snatches of old songs, the surrender. And finally – left to wonder what local custom or curious sense of purpose had caused everyone to scarper so blithely off into the bushes, leaving her, muzzy-headed and alone, in the glare of the noonday sun. Yet how lovely that jacaranda tree against that outcropping of rock, how irritating the pinch of her walking shorts just above her belly button and how like her thumbnails to her mother's when she reached up her hands to shade her eyes. How brilliant and unending the clear Spanish sky!

(What would she miss? Nobody liked slush in Toronto; it was snow's dirty cousin. But Carla did. At bus stops she used to make piles of it with the sides of her boots, then press down slowly with her heels until it flowered out squishily.

She wished she could see her brother, tap his shoulder in a crowd, have him turn around and face her. She knew what she would say. She would hold on to his arm and stay steady while she said it.)

Carla could hear them up at one of the restaurants. They had turned on the television: the news reports, the moving, fiery picture, the hush, the slack-jawed patter. There was a seagull calling out belligerently to the flapping flippers of a snorkeller. 'War, war, war,' sounded the cry to the larger, lacerated, love-soaked world. She would not tell Lisa right away. She had spotted her about twenty metres down the beach. Her niece was sitting straight-backed on the sand, a stolid, beautiful Canadian Buddha. The bad news would sniff her out, the way news, good or bad, always, eventually does.

There was a bit of a ruckus up at the restaurant, but Lisa liked the feeling of not turning her head, not needing to know. If it was serious enough, it would make its way down to this beach. She had a fleeting feeling right then, of her life stretching off – not in front of her in some winding, brambly or inconveniently forked road, but instead dispersing in every possible direction into a kind of happy mist. She could see now that the black bobbing buoy was not a buoy at all but a snorkeller, searching for something. Or maybe not searching at all. Maybe just observing. What was down there? She would buy some flippers and duck under like that. '*Ay, corazón,*' she sang softly to herself. *Ay, ay, corazón*.

YOUR ANSWER, DO

'I am not impressed,' said Daisy, slapping at the thigh of her jeans where some flour had settled. 'There's a murderer out there, Jo. What are you doing about it?'

Jo was not going to do anything. What could she do? Murderers were not like malls that you could navigate, or like ice cream vendors, who were frightening and clangy but followed a protocol. She could do nothing but push down the love for her daughter that rose in her like bile. And this, this peach pie – this she could do, although Daisy would have none of it.

'I'm going to the bar.'

Again, thought Jo, but nodded.

'I'm going to the bar to drink margaritas with the DFI's. Drunken Fucking Indians, Jo. Friends. Ever heard of them?'

Jo nodded again and pressed her thumbs deeply into the mound of dough sitting on the counter.

'Bye, then,' said Daisy, and grabbed a handful of keys and luck charms from a hook near the door. A whoosh of new-millennium hairdo and midriff, teenaged sweat and sweet ylang-ylang, and she was gone.

'Bye,' said Jo. She began to knead the dough with the heels of her hands, stopping only to sprinkle flour periodically.

Since Jo and Simon split two years ago, this had been Daisy's thing: the outrageous requests coupled with the offhand provocations. Maybe Daisy would never forgive Jo, but she still needed her. Jo picked up the rolling pin and stroked flour along its length. She understood her job now to be one of quiet bolstering. The best sort of crutch propped up its bearer woodenly, and without fuss.

When Jo was alone in the Chinatown flower shop where she worked, she would often step into the flower fridge and stand amongst the most decadent, exotic blooms, inhaling their perfumes like a rajah, as goosebumps pittered up the insides of her arms.

It should have come as no surprise, then, that when lust overtook her, it was in a great, illicit and inevitable waft; it made her feel sniffy and giddy and she could not resist it. She left her long-time lover and father of Daisy, Simon, for a man named Wallace, a Scottish journalist in town for his sister's funeral. Great white lilies, orchids and pearly roses. Not death, not only sex, but something else. Sitting on the edge of his chenille bedspread in the Royal York, she'd glimpsed another life shining like skin through rain-soaked cotton. She sat on the bed and her heart hummed. It was all so slow and precipitous. Then a second battering, slower still, and more blissful, between her legs. She wanted to fuck, but more than this she wanted to be open, on offer – not only to Wallace, but to the world, which she saw now as raw, glistening and teeming. It was the revelation of toppling an unwieldy rock as a child, coming face to face with all that sudden, scurrying, moist underside.

'I think maybe he was the love of my life,' she had said last Saturday, all silly, spritzing buds.

'People always say that about the one who got away,' said Jenny, Jo's assistant.

'Right,' said Jo.

But had he gotten away? And didn't that line of reasoning really only apply to fishing or race-car drivers?

'Let's try this,' said Jenny. *This* was a survey in *Psychology Now* to do with cultural mores. They sat on the store's stoop and, using Jenny's eyeliner, ticked the tiny squares gauging goodness. Next they had to rate their top five moral offences: from most to least odious. Jo supposed this was the kind of thing people did when the newspapers could describe only perilous options: strangers or familiars whose connectors had snapped.

Jo's list looked like this:

1   Killing your brother.
2   Sending your army to certain death.
3   Plotting to kill your child.
4   Betraying a friend.
5   Cheating on your husband/wife.

Jenny's list looked like this:

1   Insulting your mother.
2   Plotting to kill your child.
3   Sending your army to certain death.
4   Killing your brother.
5   Lying to your people.

'Let me see yours,' said Jo.

'Jo and Jenny,' said Syd, the owner, walking by. 'Two peas in a mixed-up pod.'

It was true: Jo, blonde and big-boned; Jenny, black-haired and hipless.

'How's biz?'

'Slow,' said Jenny. 'We're rating sins.'

'Ah,' said Syd, over Jo's shoulder. 'Betraying a friend. Nothing worse. A wife is one thing. A friend fields your heartache like no other. Never betray a friend. Those carnations come in?'

'Yep, they're in the backroom fridge.' Jo waved him back. 'Let's see yours,' she said again.

'Okay, swap.'

'Wow,' said Jo, 'strange choice for numero uno. And two.'

'Motherlove is the greatest love, you know. In China we have a saying: "Even a tiger will not kill her young."'

'Well. Chinese way best way. Let's go out back later and see if we can't dig our way down there with our trowels.'

'Mmm. It's too hot. Besides, I'm not sure tigers feel the same about girl babies.'

On the sidewalk in front of them, pigeons mated, jousting with tiny clacking beaks. A quick preen, then an awkward, iridescent mount.

'I did a bad thing, Jenny.'

A delivery truck roared by.

'You had great sex and you messed up your relationship. Who couldn't see that coming down the river?'

Jo gave Jenny the two-fingered *fuck you*.

Across the street a fat man walked by, holding a skinny woman's hand as if it were gloved.

'Why two?'

'The Brits captured some French archers and cut off their *doigts* in the Hundred Years War. It's a taunt.'

'Brutal.'

'Yeah, but war. I wasn't talking about Wallace. It's Daisy.'

'Gimme your answer, do.'

'I followed her to the bar the other night.'

'Jesus, Jo. You need to let go. Just trust she'll get past it.'

'It wasn't her I was worried about.'

'Oh. But.'

'There was a man, Jenny. He looked exactly like the sketch in the papers. It was dark, but I could tell.'

'What did you do?'

'I hit him with a two-by-four.'

'A two-by-four? Fuck. Other people pack heat. Is he okay? I mean, did you? Was he okay?'

'I think he's okay. I don't really care, but I think he's okay. Oh, I miss Simon. And I cannot stand Simon. Let's go inside.'

So they did, two peas in a mixed-up pod, up the stairs into Syd's Flowers, where the daffodils and hydrangeas and birds of paradise lived and died together.

Last year, for novelty's sake, Syd suggested they get into floriography. Jenny read in a snooty accent from the guidebook: *Not only love and happiness were the tenor of these floral missives; coquetry, dalliance, prevarication, indifference and coolness; rebuff, refusal, scorn, contempt and insult – all were expressed by a suitably chosen flower. Misguided zeal in trying to secure artistic effects in a floral token will entirely wreck the scheme.*

They took turns arranging wrecked schemes, plucking flowers for their clashing certainties. Clematis, Intellectuality: 'I pay tribute to your brilliance and cleverness' intertwined with Love-in-a-mist, Uncertainty: 'Your message is ambiguous; what do you mean?' Or Corn-cockle, Gentility: 'Though appearances may not suggest it, I am of gentle birth' nestled next to Monkey Musk, Coxcomb: 'I cannot tolerate a fop.'

A couple of months after Simon left, Jo and Jenny tried it, what Daisy, at the age of five, had called the 'clothes-off kind of love.' They drank three bottles of do-it-yourself Pinot Noir, ate lots of fancy pretzels and exchanged pivotal moments.

'When my brother left to go back to China,' said Jenny, 'he took me aside and told me to be brave.'

'What did you say?'

'I said, don't go. I said, it feels like thousands of tiny ants are biting at my heart. Then I threw up on his shoes.'

'That wasn't very nice.'

'No, but families.'

'Right.' Jo took another swig of wine.

'What was your biggest moment?'

'Having Daisy, of course,' said Jo, with too much resolve. Because, even then, she could not be sure. (Daisy, Temporization: 'I will give you an answer in a few days.')

And once their jeans and tees lay in colourful heaps on the floor, Jo could do nothing but weep into Jenny's pale shoulder.

'He said the warm water from his spirit would flow out to the desert of my heart,' whispered Jenny.

'Across the world?' said Jo, knowing the answer already.

'Across the world.'

And kill the ants, thought Jo, but held her thick, grape-soaked tongue. She stroked Jenny's smooth pelt of hair, but in the end she was shy, or chicken, or both. They dozed off, woke bashful, downed some coffee and dove right back into the day-to-day.

Jo pried a flattened portion of dough from the counter, then placed and pinched it carefully into the pan. Lately she felt shy with her daughter, inarticulate. Daisy's very personhood seemed strange to her, sudden and unheralded, as if she'd sprung from someone else's head, fully formed. But the night Jo followed Daisy, she had not been shy. What she had that night was a mother's clout, giant-like and arrogant. She slipped on sneakers and slipped out the back when she was sure Daisy had rounded the corner, then was momentarily unsure. How did one tail one's own child?

She made her way quickly out to Nassau Street and spotted Daisy swinging her purse on a corner. Jo hid behind a wall of boxes blotchy with fish juice. Daisy was standing in front of a cheese shop. Big blocks of Gouda and Emmenthal hunkered in the shop window. Daisy looked at her watch, shrugged, then swung her purse again. When she started up the street, Jo paused then followed. Daisy was cutting across the schoolyard, muttering. Jo crouched near a tire swing and watched Daisy roll a joint. She looked up through the hole in the tire to the sky, which was not yet dark, still ruddy with greys and dirty oranges. All of Daisy's childhood seemed sequestered in that playground: the flowery elbow scabs, the addled dreams, the deceit, the dirty, adorable dismembered dolls, the graffiti and growth spurts. Jo wanted to say something, but wouldn't. She watched Daisy. Daisy took a toke and closed her eyes, then opened them quickly, startled. Was Jo noisy in her thinking? Jo looked over her shoulder and saw some-one. Someone else, a shadow in the school's entranceway. Daisy shrugged again. It was her prerogative. Jo crouched lower and scanned the schoolyard. There was a scrap pile down the road, next to a store that sold junky jewellery and wasp-waisted dresses. Daisy was hunkered by the sandbox, the joint's light creating a dim glow around her chin. Jo scurried over to the scrap pile, dug out a piece of lumber and skirted the perimeter of the schoolyard.

Then Daisy was on the move again, striding along Spadina, the shadow close behind her. Jo followed. In the intersection, amidst the traffic, the night was muggy, abuzz with insects, insults and intentions. It was the kind of night when angry young men in navy blue hoodies peered and preened on street corners. *Why don't you go back where you came from*, they sneered at passersby with different smells and skin. Armed, Jo tried for casual. It was best to carry the board like a baby, across her breast, as she walked.

Jo combined some sugar and cornstarch in a pot, scrambled to open the can of nectar, then carefully poured the liquid over the sweet mess. She found some bottled lemon juice at the back of the fridge, and decided to forego the lemon rind. The mix began to warm and thicken as she stirred.

When Daisy turned into an alley, and the shadow after, Jo had closed the distance between them. The shadow drew closer to Daisy. Jo drew closer to the shadow. Daisy pulled the joint from her pocket and looked at her watch again. The shadow skulked behind a dumpster.

Jo took the pot off the stove and spooned the glaze into a bowl, then cleared a space in the fridge. She would have to wait for it to chill.

It would not be unfair to say she felt a brief flash of kinship with Daisy's stalker – his absolute nerve! – before she brought the board down heavily onto his shoulder and he fell to his knees. She lifted the board again and paused for only a second to sneak a look at her daughter before she swung it horizontally once more across the kneeling man's head. Just like T-ball, she mused. Same height, same rickety straight posture. Out in the laneway, Daisy was getting safely stoned, and Jo was glad. But when she saw the shadow sprawled, with the sudden patch of red shining through the hair on his scalp, she sobered. 'Rusty nail,' she thought out loud. *He'll need a tetanus shot when he wakes up.* And, unbidden: Simon would be proud of me.

Simon was a jazz musician; he played guitar at several clubs around town, always with his eyes closed. When they first started dating, Jo would go to all of the gigs, sit by herself, sip at red wine and wish that she smoked. Mostly, she was the only woman in a cluster of men, their fingers small rhythmic animals snapping in their laps. Jo would close her eyes too, hoping that by shutting out the sight of so many busy fingers and intent faces she could come closer to the mystery of the music itself. Instead she saw only the prohibitive black lines of a music staff striped across her eyelids, with carefree-looking quarter notes nestling in the spaces, daring her to decipher them. Sometimes she focused on the tapping of Simon's foot, the heel-toe certainty of it. She watched the way it caused the room to move, the huge upside-down U-lights of the candles undulating on the walls above the tables like dancing gods. Later, Simon might invite some of his friends back to their dollhouse of a bungalow near Kensington Market, where they lounged in a scattered semicircle, passed a joint and listened to some tunes, the smoky sweet air and the strains of a saxophone player wreathing their tousled heads. 'Heavy, man,' they'd say. 'He's a really heavy player.'

Daisy was a happy accident. 'You're a love child, baby,' she told her, when at eleven she waxed curious. 'No glove, no love,' replied her lackadaisical progeny. 'You don't make sense,' said Jo. 'Oh, yes I do,' said Daisy.

First, Jo had left them both. 'Meet me in Italy,' Wallace said, and she jetted off to Florence. For two days he was preoccupied and purposeful with conferences and documents. An Italian soldier followed Jo through the Uffizi Gallery until she gave in and kissed him outside, in the shadow of a fountain. 'I felt like a postcard,' she explained to Wallace later, wonderingly. 'I've never felt like a post-card.' They stayed in bed for four days, and he told her amazing stories about herself while he was inside her. How did he know? On the seventh day there were more conferences, and when Wallace came back to the hotel room, Jo was asleep. She woke to him stroking her Caesarean scar with his thumb, sighing, 'You're a mother.' She kept her eyes closed. There was a scenario in his sigh, and the scenario involved Jo, her child and her guilt. The sigh coddled Jo's guilt as if the guilt itself were a child. Wallace knew that Jo would leave, and because he knew, she left the next morning, wordlessly, feeling complicitous and unclean.

She went back to Simon and Simon left her. Made love to her, made her come while she cried, and walked out the door with his guitar flung sideways across his back.

Wallace, childless, had asked her about Daisy over a room-service dinner the last night.

'I watched her fall once,' said Jo. 'My sister Kate was babysitting her best friend's five-year-old, so we went to the park together. Daisy was seven months old.'

Wallace nodded for longer than was really necessary, which both annoyed and comforted Jo. *Seven months old,* he seemed to be saying. *When they're that young you have to count in months.*

'I was still breastfeeding, but Daise was getting interesting. You know, her face moved, and she made her own special noises, but she still couldn't roll all by herself. We spread a blanket under a tree near the wading pool. It was so humid and rank. Toronto in August. Lola, Kate's charge, was a real live wire, oblivious to the heat, oblivious to us, really. But Daisy she loved. We helped her to help Daisy roll from one side to another. It cheered us, you know. A roly-poly baby and a smiley, pigtailed kid in cut-offs. Lola went for a swim in the wading pool and I sat with Daisy on a bench to watch her. Then Kate took a turn with Daise while I paddled. Lola wanted Daisy to swim so she ran over to Kate and pulled her from her lap. Just like that. They fell together, so it was cushy. But Daisy cried and cried and cried.'

Wallace was looking at Jo as if he'd just been handed a golden egg.

'I blamed myself, and then I blamed Lola. And Lola blamed Daisy. Do you believe it – she was a baby, for Chrissakes! And Kate blamed herself. And we were all so worried. I've told Daisy that story so many times, and once she said she thought she remembered Kate's sundress, but that was all.'

'Strange what affects us and what flows over us,' said Wallace. 'I've noticed that in war zones. What we in the West like to call post-traumatic stress is just life to other people.'

Jo could not tell if Wallace was joking, and, at that moment, she couldn't bring herself to care. She liked him because he used so many words in so many combinations, and his journalism training made him alert and constantly curious, like a squirrel. She liked him also because she could tell he saw her life like a feature article. He gave it some shape. Simon used the same words over and over again. He was frugal with words.

After Simon left, she was light-headed for days, rocketing from room to room of the dollhouse, dragging the tips of her fingers along the walls, fixing Daisy elaborate lunches – devilled eggs and dainty watercress sandwiches, or untidy nouvelle cuisine wraps with cilantro hanging like lace out the ends. Then, it was true, for a while there, she did not really notice her daughter.

When Daisy was nine and Simon on tour, the police raided their home. They busted in the front door and clomped up to Daisy's room first – plainclothes, guns unsheathed in their fat-fingered hands, they stood in her doorway and glowered like men from a fairy tale full of inbreds. When Jo padded up to them, they were already deflated, done in by the small girl in Spiderman pyjamas who sat, wakeful, silent, still. They left the doors swinging saloon-like on their busted hinges, tutting something about *gambling ring* and *address mix-up* into the quiet and hoisting their pants above their privileged hips. Jo tried to hold Daisy, but Daisy refused.

'Who will fix the doors?' she said.

Jo tried to lift her from the bed.

'Don't,' said Daisy.

'Oh,' said Jo. Then, 'We'll have to wash the sheets.' The stain was mustard-coloured. Like baby shit. She felt ashamed.

Of herself or Daisy? 'We'll wash them, honey,' she said, and drew Daisy close.

'We'll burn them,' her slumped, stone-faced child had pronounced. 'Right after we fix the doors.'

The recipe called for three pounds of firm ripe peaches, peeled and thickly sliced. Speaking this aloud made Jo think of a storybook, one of Daisy's old favourites, where a boy cannot help but say things twice. This is something the adults in his life do not indulge; it gets to be annoying after a while. But Daisy had never been bothersome that way.

They'd had a discussion once, the bunch of them, about the viability of a fetus and the Supreme Court. It got heated and loud, the way these things do. Jo's sister Kate started using the *cunt* word, as in *my goddamn cunt*, and Jenny began bellowing belligerently in Cantonese. Jo envied them the courage of their convictions. She herself felt wavery, unresolved.

'Maybe Daisy shouldn't be hearing this,' said Simon, which made Kate splutter and spiral into indignation. Daisy, aged seven, was playing with bits of yarn and two squat people she'd fashioned from thumbtacks and used wine corks.

'She's okay, she's playing,' said Jenny.

'Leave her,' said Kate. 'You're playing, right, sweetheart?'

Jo got up, then sat down again beside Daisy. It was the least she could do.

'Honey?' she said.

Daisy laid the cork people side by side, surveying the larger, real people before she spoke. 'Why does *he* get to decide?'

They were silent, considering.

Jo was the one who asked. 'Who, honey?'

'The *goat*, mom. Why does the supreme goat get to decide?'

And to that question none of them truly had the answer.

Simon sang to Daisy that night, accompanying himself softly, stooped over his instrument, stooped over his sleepyheaded girl. *I'm half crazy over the love of you. It won't be a fancy marriage. I can't afford a carriage ...*

Jo fetched the cooled pie shell down from the shelf next to the stereo, then arranged some of the sliced peaches in it and went to check on the glaze. It was still lukewarm.

On the way home from the two-by-four incident, Jo had passed some of Daisy's DFI's on the street, huddled together for heat. She stopped and said hello.

'You look like a nice girl who likes to have a lot of fun,' said a man with a bandaged eye.

Jo nodded.

'Canada's a good country, isn't it? A progressive country, good for the young people.'

'Yes.'

The bandaged-eye man pulled a rolled sheet of paper from his bundle. On the paper was a photocopy of a sketch done in what looked to be black marker. It was a gypsy woman, large hoops dangling from her delicate ears, her hair dark and upswept, long eyelashes casting shadows on her cheeks.

'It's nice,' said Jo. 'She's beautiful.'

'Three dollars,' said the man, holding out his palm.

Jo passed him some coins and he laughed.

'You know, you got a good deal. The originals go for thirty-five bucks. If you buy me tea I could maybe give you one.'

'Did you buy an original?' said Jenny, playing with the cash register.

'No, I went home.'

'You're a bit of a loony, Jo.'

'Huh,' said Jo. (Clarkia, Pleasure: 'Your company and converse delight me.') 'Did you know Simon has a gig in the Jazz Fest? Daisy left the flyer out for me.'

'Jo, you don't love Simon. You love whatever's Simon in Daisy, and you're lonely.'

'I know. It feels like thousands of tiny ants are biting at my heart.'

Jo and Simon had first met in a crowded hardware store on Spadina as she strained to reach lightbulbs stacked on the top shelf. When her fingers finally reached the edge of the lowest box, she felt the stack begin to teeter and closed her eyes in anticipation of the tinkle of frosted glass and filament on linoleum. Instead, she was treated to a showbiz-like 'Ta-dah!' from a tall bearded man in whose arms the lightbulbs were precariously balanced. They went for coffee and peach pie at a local café. Simon made jokes about how Jo lit up his life. Jo supposed it was the sort of story made for family legend.

Now, when Simon came to call, he stood at attention on the front lawn at the appointed hour. Daisy skipped down the walk, the two of them tipped their insolent faces quickly towards the house, then zoomed off together like a gang, which they were.

'Why not Poinsettia or Iris even?' Daisy, aged twelve, had asked.

Eager, hollow-hearted Jo: 'I wanted things to be uncomplicated for you. I wanted you to have a clear-spirited gladness and a small, focused centre.' Bullshit. She wanted her life to be simple. Daisy: long-lasting and hardy, oblivious to tending.

Jo tried not to keep cut flowers at home. It was enough to be among the raw, amputated stems in her working day; at night she allowed only the green gasps of houseplants to whisper in on her dreams. But sometimes, when she couldn't sleep, or some city sound had jolted her from slumber, she would get up and dig her fingers into the soil of her potted azalea, just to feel the richness, the rootedness, the loamy love of it.

Jo fetched the glaze from the fridge again and found it sufficiently cold. She poured some of it into the pie shell, distributed the remaining peach slices, then poured more glaze on top. The whole pie would have to chill now for at least two hours. She sighed and sat down to wait. Daisy had been wearing nail polish when she left, a new development. Jo had watched her daughter as she leaned up against the counter and tapped on the lid of a jar of salsa with one pointy nail painted silver like a fish scale.

Daisy and Jo had the sex talk early, when Daisy skipped home wearing a necklace of silvery packaged condoms, slick and accessible, like candy.

'Pride Parade,' said Simon soulfully.

When boys started sniffing around, Jo tried again.

'I'm not having sex, Jo,' said Daisy, fourteen. 'I've seen what it does to people.'

Jo nodded like a sage. Abortion, adoption, disease: so many things to struggle for and against.

'It stupefies them, Jo. Stupefaction, that's the definition of sex, and, frankly, I don't care for it.'

And Jo had put it down to posturing, the kind of teenaged posturing that makes you rock right back on your heels in admiration. When she told Simon, he smiled and said, 'Our good, strange girl, eh?'

Now, with a murderer on the loose, Jo wished for nothing more than a Daisy that pedantic, that chillingly wise.

Jo opened the fridge and tapped her knuckle lightly on the glaze. It was still gooey. She turned on the small television set in the corner and there was the news. A man ran screaming through foreign streets, the blood on his clothes not his own. Then, for a moment, a woman with curvy yellow hair and a taut, innocent brow sat behind a protective desk and talked about outbreaks and cycles. Next, four families, grinning and grateful, began moving their furniture into houses built for them by strangers. Jo began to cry. The yellow-haired woman came back and told her not to worry, that the police had a suspect in custody. Jo still worried. She opened the fridge door and looked at the pie again, which appeared no more chilled than five minutes ago. This will take forever, she thought.

Until, there she was. Daisy, back from the bar, big in the kitchen. Important like an airplane, rife with flight and precious pieces to be maintained. (Purple Columbine, Resolve: 'I shall never give you up.')

'So?' Daisy pointed to the television.

Jo ran her fingers through her hair in a humble way, although it was Daisy she wanted to touch. 'I baked a peach pie,' she said.

Daisy opened the fridge and peered inside. 'Yes, you did.'

'It's chillin',' said Jo. Was Daisy smiling?

'Right. What about the murderer?'

'They caught someone.' Jo gestured vaguely towards the TV. 'But, you know, crooks, do-gooders, entertainers … That's the way of the world. The bad guys just float to the surface like bad eggs.'

'My ass, Mom.'

This from Jo's gorgeous, near-grown daughter. Gorgeous, going on seventeen, wrong and so, so right. Jo sized up Daisy as she poured herself some cranberry juice and chugged it down. She had her father's toothpick legs and square jaw, but still couldn't cope with breasts. She rounded her shoulders around them like she'd been punched, or was hugging someone strange and blameless and invisible. When she'd finished the juice, she placed the glass gently in the sink and turned back towards her mother.

'My ass,' she said again, and looked Jo bang in the eye.

THE CAPTAIN'S NAME WAS NED

Dad said Kyra had legs like tree trunks and a mouth like a rip in a mattress. So that when she came marching out of the parkette at the top of our street, as she did nearly every Thursday that summer, I imagined her knees uprooting her feet with every step, and strained to make out the pink flap above her chin. I was nine years old and had taken to squinting the meaning into things. I could sit on our front porch for hours, with only the street's unplanned procession for entertainment. I got it down to an art, to the point where the crinkled contours of a paper bag became the dark form of a lurking rodent, the waving of distant tree limbs the beckoning of a woman dressed too posh and pretty for summer in the city. People became moving pieces of the landscape, to be acknowledged only by stilted nods. Kyra was the exception.

'You doing anything today, Maddie?'

She had spotted me and was careening down the street in anticipation. I stood up.

'No.' I was never really doing anything that summer. My brother had just returned from Scout camp.

'Collected kindling,' he said, when Mum asked. She signed him up for remedial math for the remainder of July.

I had refused gymnastics, with its convoy of compact leotarded bodies, and macramé. I wanted the two long months to myself. And they were long, with no marked weekends to rein the weeks in. When I wasn't on the porch, I sat in the weak spray of the lawn sprinkler, gazing fitfully at my shins and sucking on sunflower seeds. The tar on the street mellowed then melted, and the days pitter-pattered forward like centipede feet.

As Kyra approached, I noticed her T-shirt was soaked through under the arms, two lopsided clammy patches stretching over to her breasts.

'You're sweating,' I said lamely. Her woman's body still blindsided me every so often with its effusions.

'Yeah, so what?' She sat down beside me. 'Let's go to the park.'

The park was the largest of its kind in the city, replete with pooping, strutting Canada geese, peanut-fattened squirrels and punched-in soccer balls – a tract of green, treed land that stretched like surprise between Lake Ontario and the bisecting main street. In the summer it had strollers and dogs and a mini zoo with antelopes and peacocks, wood-chip paths and an orange girder sculpture that rose irrationally from the earth. To the south, bordered by the highway, was a pond that froze frothily in early winter, then hardened to a cloudy emerald in January. If you jumped on the ice then, you could hear it: the echo of water beneath as it rolled and shifted and broke on a deep, distant shoal. But summertime on the pond meant ducks and swans and paper sailboats, and a boundless dry-eyed sky reflecting back at you.

Kyra had a bag of bread crusts in her pocket. She passed me some, and we tossed them to the ducks, who scrabbled and quacked.

'There's a thousand dead soldiers at the bottom of the pond,' I told her, 'dead as doornails, all of them.'

'Did they sink?'

'No,' I said, 'they fell. It was in the dead of winter, and they were fighting the enemy.'

'Who was the enemy?'

I couldn't remember who the enemy was, could not even remember if the soldiers themselves were French or English or American. They were not Indians, because they had big brass buttons on their coats, this much I knew.

'The enemy was very intelligent. They knew the soldiers had to get to the lake, so they forced them to walk across the ice.' I pitched a crust out into the middle of the pond and we watched it sink. 'The ice was not thick enough yet to hold them. It cracked right down the middle, and they fell through the crack, never to be seen again.'

'I saw them,' Kyra said, 'I saw them in a movie. Their faces were all swelled up.'

'Did not see them.'

'Did too.' She shook the remaining crumbs from the bag onto the grass. A Canada goose flopped its long neck over my knee to nibble them. The grass beside me had dried to a beige stubble.

'Let's go to the playground,' I said.

The goose charged at Kyra, who grunted and swatted at its head. 'Stupid asshole,' she shouted, and several mothers turned chidingly.

'Geese can't be assholes,' I whispered.

'Where's your brother?' she asked. 'My brother never visits. He lives in Winnipeg and carries a briefcase. Look at that red bird, it looks like a piece of blood in the sky. Do you get the blood, the monthlies? I think you're too young. You're just a kid.'

It was necessary, in Kyra's presence, to let whole phrases unspool, uncensored. Sometimes, if you followed them, they took you somewhere, but mostly they just streamed out and away.

The first time I met Kyra I hid. Her voice reminded me of the undersides of bridges, the trolls who hunkered there. We were in the kitchen, Mum, Dad and I. My brother was outside playing street hockey when she arrived, her parents in tow. I crouched behind a chair to listen.

'She saw an old wedding photo with you in it and wanted to visit,' her mother said, and stayed standing, sentinel-like, to one side of her.

Kyra's hands were everywhere. First on her person, patting at her pockets, at her high mounded breasts, then on the table, picking up a salt shaker, the Canadian Tire catalogue. I watched as she lifted the Weetabix box from the cupboard, shook it next to her ear and fished out the free figurine, tucking it into the waistband of her pants. She was stealing! I felt something humming inside of me, a notion of what was actually possible.

I asked Mum about the wedding photo later that night.

'Bridesmaid, or some such thing. Horrible lime-green poufy dress,' she said, a book laid bare in her lap. 'Don't you ever do that,' she added, and placed her finger under a word on the page.

'So much fuss ...' She shook her head, and I understood I had been advised of something that may or may not become clear to me in the future.

'Kyra, though, nice girl, bit bullheaded.' The book still prone, the word still waiting.

'Pole-skee, Pole-skee, pass me the pierogies,' was what Kyra had chanted on the way to the park as we passed the delis and bakeries on Roncesvalles. 'If you're good later, maybe I'll buy us some kielbasa.' She saluted to the statue of the pope on the corner and swiped a chunk of sausage in a deli two stores down.

The only part of kielbasa I liked was peeling away the thin layer of skin, exposing the insides, which were thick and striated, like an overfed earthworm.

'You know what it looks like,' Kyra said, and bit off a chunk.

The pearly pieces of fat embedded in the pink nauseated me, but I was interested in the fact that someone had taken the time to put them there.

Kyra took my hand and held it, her walnut knuckles white with the effort.

'You smell like asparagus piss,' I said.

'Asparaguses don't piss. They're a vegetable, asshole.'

'No, you smell like piss does after you eat asparagus. And girls can't be assholes.'

'Why not?'

'Because they just can't. They have to be whores or bitches or sluts.'

'You're still an asshole.' She dropped my hand.

I put the kielbasa skin in my pocket for safekeeping.

When we reached the playground, Kyra laughed out loud at the sighing of the swings. She began to push the children, running between the small bums tucked like dumplings so that they maintained the same dizzying height. The children started to keen meekly, their sobs caught in the whoosh and sway. That was when the mothers came scurrying, mouths snagged for a second between well-meaning and worry.

'Not so hard, honey, you can't push them so hard.' A hand on Kyra's shoulder, a glance at me, hanging from the A of the swing set, my legs thrashing with the effort of the climb.

Kyra swore under her breath, and I moved on to the slide, with poor results, the backs of my thighs sticking like raw chicken to the metal. We grabbed handfuls of gravel from the ground and threw them down the ramp. There was pleasure in the wild skittering sound and the white dust that dried smoothly on our palms.

'I'm going to die, you know.' Kyra brushed her hands on her jean shorts. 'It's how it is with us, because we have an extra chromosome.' This, proudly. 'That's why I don't run so much, because my heart is weak.'

'I thought running made your heart stronger, farthead.' I had been suckered by Kyra's theories before.

'No, it makes it go faster, and use up more beats, and when you die, it's because you used up the beats you got when you were born.' She threw some gravel at me.

Dad invited Kyra to stay for supper.

'Yes,' said Mum, 'stay.'

Supper was pork chops, mashed potatoes and salad with Thousand Island dressing that slid quickly from the bottle. Kyra was the first to finish. She put her knife and fork down on her unused serviette and wandered over to the window.

'Could you pass the totties, Maddie?' Dad said.

I slid the dish across the table.

Dad tapped two potato clods onto his plate. 'How was school, Jeremy?'

'Tore up my elbow at recess,' said my brother, and held up his arm, which was cross-hatched with scrapes.

'What about the learning part?'

'Test. Roy got caught cheating. I stayed in after school with him.'

'As long as you didn't do the cheating. Solidarity.' Dad scanned the sky, then turned to Kyra. 'Enough blue out there to make a Dutchman a pair of pants, eh?'

Kyra grunted but did not speak. There was a group of sparrows pecking at some seeds in the garden, jerking their heads like tiny apostrophes. The last of the roses were in full bloom; their scent wafted slovenly through the back door. I couldn't finish my pork chop.

'Tsk, tsk, you're always last,' said Mum.

'Ach, if you come in last, at least you come in ahead of all those poor sods who never started.' Dad made a face at the pork chop.

'That's the problem with you, Gordon, you never start.' Clanging and rearranging.

Dad went to sit beside Kyra on the couch, to watch the birds. 'Never mind then, never mind,' he muttered. 'Could you fix me a drink, Reenie? My mouth's as dry as an Arab's sandshoe.' He turned to Kyra. 'Birds are funny, aren't they?'

'Why?'

'Well, they've no arms. None at all.' He got up then and began to dance, his arms clutched behind his back, his chin thrust forward in an attempt at a beak.

My brother shook his head. 'That's because they have wings.' He slammed his glass down on the table.

Dad pursed his lips, then began to sing.

> *Ye cannae shove yer grannie off the bus,*
> *Oh, ye cannae shove yer grannie off the bus,*
> *Ye cannae shove yer grannie,*
> *For she's your mammy's mammy,*
> *Ye cannae shove yer grannie off the bus!*

He grabbed Mum by the waist and swung her around the kitchen until a laugh galloped out of her.

Singing I will if you will, so will I!
Singing I will if you will, I will if you will,
I will if you will, so will I!

Later, Kyra and I watched my father, followed his movements as he prepared to go out with my mother. First the hair: a quick comb in the upstairs bathroom, then downstairs to the kitchen where he stood, head bent forward over the boiling kettle, trying to banish static from the few flyaway hairs that still sprouted from his forehead. Back upstairs to the bathroom, a quick slap of aftershave, one, two, behind the ears, on the sinewed sides of neck.

'I've still got it, eh, Reenie, I've still got it!'

Downstairs again, distracted, to the front closet for the vacuum, which sputtered and shook, snarky with overuse. Back and forth, back and forth across the foyer in wide sweeping arcs that left trails, a wake in the maroon shag carpet. Finally, sitting at the organ.

Those were the days, my friend,
We thought they'd never end!

Until my mother was waiting in the hallway in her high heels, and they left together to wait on the porch for the babysitter, with a two-tiered shudder of the door.

The babysitter arrived as Kyra was leaving. Stephanie was tall and chesty, with tight black jeans and a Vancouver Canucks sweatshirt. Her features were plain and widely spaced under her high cheerleader's ponytail, giving her the look of a well-intentioned frog.

'Hiya,' Kyra said, and held out her hand.

'Hi. How are you? I'm Stephanie.' Stephanie gave Kyra her hand, with its moulting purple nails, then pulled away. As she passed Kyra she blew a slick, slow-motion bubble with her gum, allowed it to float there like a heavenly sphere, then sucked the gum in, quick and coordinated. There was a gold comb sticking out of her back pocket. I watched as Kyra slid it smoothly out and dropped it into her plastic bag. Then, *ba-dunk, ba-dunk*, the swing of her wide hips, all the way up the street.

Our mother would not allow bubble gum in the house, on account of the mess, but Stephanie pulled a pack from her red vinyl purse.

'I'll teach you,' she said.

Jeremy looked up, as if trolling for something in his eyebrows, but stayed.

We practised for forty-five minutes, until the gum had gone plasticky. My brother pinched me hard, then went to his room. Stephanie let me watch TV with her, in my pyjamas, sitting close to the screen. She shared her popcorn and explained the back-stories of a show about drilling for oil and having affairs in Dallas. When the late-night movie came on we both sat, hushed, fixed to the glow by a young girl possessed by the devil, her skin all of a sudden pockmarked, her words Satanic spitballs. She's like Kyra, I thought.

'She's like Kyra.'

Stephanie hooked her ponytail elastic with her index finger, then shook out her hair as if she were about to have an affair.

'That is really mean, Maddie. Retarded means slow, not stopped. You should feel sorry for her. Not be making fun of her.' Stephanie threw up the ends of her sentences like juggling balls. I could tell she thought it was my job to catch them.

Advice, I thought.

Stephanie snapped her gum and stretched so that her sweat-shirt rode up above the coiled bud of her belly button. Then she yawned and looked at her watch. 'It's really past your bedtime.'

Once, when I was only two, and Jeremy was four, I watched him shadow our regular babysitter, Gwen, around the house, ducking behind doors and squatting under tables. I was there when he finally had her where he wanted her, back to him, over the sink, washing dishes. Gwen was a fleshy woman, with a rear end that protruded like a shelf for doodads, Dad said. Jeremy's face reached nearly to the top of the shelf, so that when he lifted his chin and opened his mouth, I understood immediately what was about to happen. She screamed when he bit her and locked him in his room for the rest of the afternoon. When my mother questioned him, he shrugged, serene, small. Sometimes boredom and childhood twist like hard twine inside you, until there is nothing for it but an ill-advised insurgence.

I inched closer to the screen, so that the demon girl's face was nearly touching mine through the glass.

'You're gonna be in big shit when your parents get home.' Stephanie sat up, then tucked her legs, neat like noodles, beneath her.

I was pleased to see how her bangs had matted to her head where she'd been leaning against the couch. What I felt for Stephanie was a sturdy, if temporary, hatred, useful for the way it hardened my will. I felt as a soldier must, pure in my motivations. I would not go to bed.

'When you are watching someone, you must always follow the flinching of their fingers, the machinations of their mannered faces.' Dad had discovered Kyra had been stealing things. 'Oh, yes, Maddie, you've got to watch very carefully.' He made a telescope with his hands, scanned a faraway horizon. 'I see no ships.' He patted me on the shoulder.

I took my post on the front porch, waited for Kyra's arrival, then shadowed her around the house. Before, I had smudged and splintered her movements, eyes narrowed and wary, but now I catalogued, wide-eyed and conscientious. I scrutinized as she stepped into the living room, her step ponderous, eyes snapping into place like the hands of a clock that clicks forward resolutely every five minutes. A photo of my father as a young boy (arms crossed, smile unassailable), a tiny detailed figurine (shepherd or milkmaid), a brass bell that clanged its annunciation when she picked it up.

'Kyra,' I said, 'come outside. We can play 7-Up.'

'No, you go, I'll be along soon.' Like a grandmother she said it.

I sat on the back porch and played with a piece of string, my fingers plucking at the patterns, loosening the loops, dropping then pinching, until I held a series of diamonds fast between my thumbs and forefingers. I shifted the pattern so that I could gaze through it, over the fence and into the adjoining backyard, and centred the neighbour's cat in one of the diamonds. A new method of tracking.

When Kyra came out I had moved on to the sky, trapping and tidying the clouds.

'Let me try.' She grabbed the string so that it undid itself, a mess of grubby pink lines in her open palm.

'I wouldn't mind dying,' she said, 'except there's no food in heaven. There's pop, but no food.'

I looked at her, with her square flat face, her bottom teeth shoved forward like an animal's, the label of her T-shirt lolling out the back. And our same hair, pageboy brown, hers clipped to the side with a blue plastic barrette.

'Here.' I took the string and rewove the pattern, then placed the whole thing carefully onto her stubby fingers, our hands caught for a few seconds, like double parentheses, in the web.

'You weren't watching.'

When I came back from walking Kyra up the street, Dad was standing in the doorway. I slit my eyes and tried to push past him. Mum stood behind, one hand clutching the doorknob. She took me by the shoulder and nudged me into the kitchen. There was a pot on the stove with potatoes in it.

'Sit down,' Dad said.

Several trinkets had gone missing: a farm-boy figurine, a tiny silver thimble, a photo of my parents on honeymoon in Paris, kissing, with the caption *Ooh-la-la*.

'Weren't you watching her, Mad?' His voice soft now, forgiving or forgetful.

'Yes.' I had been.

'Then how could you have missed it?'

'I dunno.' I looked at my hands, yearned for the string.

'You. Don't. Know.'

'She's a retard! Why don't you just leave her alone!'

Dad raised his arm and I saw Mum reach for something new to clutch.

I felt it then: a spaciousness in my sinuses like turning a somersault in the pool without noseplugs, a certainty. It was as if all the possibilities in my world had been narrowed down, sifted for their essence, and I was left staring, unsurprised, at what was left in the sieve.

But he didn't hit me.

'You're about as bright as a blackout.'

I closed my eyes.

When I opened them, Mum had punctured a potato with a dessert fork. 'Supper's ready,' she said.

I found my father in his workshop, standing over a pile of sawdust, a black-bristled brush in his hand, dripping Varathane like honey. He had an old housecoat belt tied around his head to keep the sweat from his face, and there were tears in his eyes. He was singing.

> *Well, the captain's name was Ned*
> *And he died just for a maid,*
> *Her name it was cried Pretty Peggy-o.*

The floor in the basement was unfinished, a hard and humped foundation. I made my way back to the storeroom, where the exposed insulation on the ceiling glowed like someone's insides. There was an empty shelf above the camping gear. If you stepped on the cooler, you could lever yourself up and sit there.

> *Captain Cook was making soup,*
> *His wife was making jelly.*
> *Captain Cook fell in the soup*
> *And burned his rubber belly.*

I had some thoughts then, questions and concerns. The captain's name was Ned, and he had died. All because of Pretty Peggy-o. This was a shifty thing. Less shifty, but no less unsettling, was the other captain's rubber belly. How many captains? And what to do with the steady golden drip of the Varathane, the sawdust and the tears?

When I approached the workshop for the second time, the singing had stopped.

'Well, that's just like you, isn't it, chittering away in the corner, looking like the ragged end of nowhere … ' He seemed to be railing at the sawhorse.

'Dad?'

The workshop was a dim, cluttered room, with a burlap cloth tacked to the wall, covered in hundreds of badges and pins. *Quebec, Je t'aime*, one read. There was one window above the main work table. It was a small, mullioned window, of the type you might see in institutions. Through the window, passing by, were the fat bottoms of two marauding raccoons, then the thin, purposeful calves and shining shoes of Lucas Stanislowski, our neighbour to the left.

My father seemed not to have noticed the driveway goings-on. If he had noticed me, he did not let on. He gave a two-by-four a pat. 'You watch yourself now, he can be mean as a snake, he can, mean as a snake.' He brought his hand up to his mouth and pantomimed a pair of fangs.

The captain's name was Ned.

I climbed the stairs.

So many songs, and so many seeming non sequiturs. These were mysteries not to be plumbed. Still, there were certain axioms in my father's universe that were impossible to counter or challenge. The captain's name was Ned: I understood this to be one of them. This was the life that had been flung upon us; we could not shake it.

Kyra's mum and dad came over the next morning, skittish with apology. My parents sat them in the living room and closed the door. My father had asked me to be there as a witness, and his temperament seemed mild, if slightly misinformed. He offered Kyra's dad a drink, but Kyra's dad was not a drinker.

'Soda,' he said, in a voice I could barely hear over the chugging of the air conditioner, 'if you have it.'

Kyra's parents were delicate, with shallow, perpetually inquisitive foreheads. Her father worried at a thread hanging from his sweater and cocked his left nostril periodically. Her mother had neck tendons that stretched like gum from her ears to her shoulders. She patted the couch and laughed at Dad's jokes. He told the one about the obscene clone fall, a shaggy-dog play on words about an out-of-control Frankenstein creature who ran through the streets swearing at little old ladies.

'And there's a bang on the mad scientist's door ... Bang! Bang! Bang! And damned if it isn't two burly policemen standing there.' He cleared his throat like a law enforcer. 'I'm sorry to inform you, Mr., Mr. ... Inventor, that you are under arrest. We have to take you in.'

'Kyra has been stealing from us,' said Mum, to get the ball rolling.

'Yes, yes, they're not valuable things, but they are precious in their own way,' Dad added.

'We've tried talking to her, but she doesn't seem to understand. We're wondering if maybe there's something else we should be doing ...'

'Yes, she's a fine girl, but the sticky fingers, the sticky fingers are a problem.' Dad gulped at his drink. 'Maddie, what do you think?'

I didn't know what I thought, except that I was aware, at that moment, of being somehow bigger than all of them, and it occurred to me that Kyra's parents, especially, looked inauthentic and naive, as if Kyra had birthed them, instead of the opposite.

When we were toddlers, Dad played a game with me and Jeremy. He lay on his back and made seats for us, his elbows rooted, his square palms bent backwards. We sat on those twin stools and he sang. At the end of every song there was a question. It was a quiz.

C'mon down the stairs, Pretty Peggy, my dear,
C'mon down the stairs, Pretty Peggy-o.
C'mon down the stairs, let down your golden hair,
Take a fair measure of your laddie-o.

'Now, Madeline, could you please tell me where, if I was to look, I would find Mount Kilimanjaro?'

The answers were not as relevant as our attitudes towards the questions. We were pre-kindergarten, after all. Still, any hesitation meant the stools, like tricky trapdoors, did not hold, and our tail-bones would drop definitively to the floor.

I considered my father's question. I considered my father. In comparison, Kyra seemed straightforward, stolid: an example.

'I think she left her galoshes here,' I said.

Dad frowned, then went out into the hallway. He came back a moment later, galoshes in hand, shaking the rubbery forms in the air so that they trembled cartoonishly. They were huge, at least five centimetres longer than his own scuffed loafers.

'I'll say one thing for Kyra.' He smiled. 'She's got a good grip on Canada, she does.' He hummed and did a little jig.

That afternoon, after Kyra's parents had left, Mum discovered Kyra had also stolen a bundle of cheques with rubber bands wound round them that Dad had tucked in the butter compart-ment of the refrigerator.

'What a bandit,' Dad said, shaking his head, 'what a bandit.'

It was decided later, by phone, that Kyra would be grounded until she found a way to pay the money back.

But at that moment, her parents just sat on the couch, looking dim and duped.

On the day Dad died, Mum, Jeremy and I sat on that same couch like a row of oversized birds. For some time we did not speak, our hearts limned with the fact of it. Then Mum twitched her arms at her sides.

'Fancy a person up and dying like that.' She mulled this over. '*Fancy* a person up and *dying* like that.'

Jeremy and I left her with a clucking group of neighbours and a battery of casserole dishes, the plastic wrap taut, opaque with steam.

We went for a walk around the block, then veered off towards the park instinctively. At the streetcar loop Jeremy stopped.

'When I was a kid, I used to think the sound of the streetcars going past was like the sound of the night breathing. Big raspy breaths, y'know?'

'Mmm,' I said, but I thought this an affected observation, unlike my brother, and I resented the choked reminiscence of his tone. I had not seen him for six months, since he moved to Hamilton to work in the steel mill. I was in my last year of high school and had just finished my university applications. I did not want to be held back.

'Hoity-toity, eh?' Dad had said when I showed him my choices. 'Well, good for you, I guess, good for you.'

The park was scabby with winter; the snow rose in dirt-flecked mounds along the trail and had frozen in some places to crunchy ice. But the trees were how I liked them best, stripped down, showing themselves against the sky.

'How was the drive?' I asked, when we reached the edge of the pond.

'Fine, bit slippery.'

We began to make our way out onto the pond surface, sliding our feet tentatively.

'I'll call Auntie Joan and the cousins. Maybe you can call about the cremation, how that all works.'

'I think he should be buried, have a proper burial.' He said this formally, like an affronted army officer.

I bounced on the ice, looked out towards the lake, across the highway. The sky over the water was a clear grey broth. 'Kyra used to say if you were really mad at a dead person, you could just stomp on his grave. Do you remember Kyra?'

'Sure,' Jeremy said, 'she used to beat me up.'

'She did?' I said, and turned towards him, although asking it aloud made me realize how much I already knew, and would know, peripherally, perennially, about Kyra, about all of us, and the versions we had been dealt.

I watched my brother begin to cry, the tears like perspiration appearing suddenly on his cheeks.

He tripped me then, sent me sprawling onto the ice so that my head hit hard, and pinned me down. He grabbed one of my arms and began slapping me across the face with my own hand. 'Hey, why're you hitting yourself? Why're you hitting yourself?' When he let me up, we were both shaking.

'I'll ask Mum about the cremation,' I said, and pulled my scarf up over my mouth.

Jeremy grabbed his cigarettes from his hip pocket and pinched one from the pack. I stood in front of him, back to the wind, and made a house for his lighter with my hands.

'Kyra,' he said, and blew out a line of steady, streamlined smoke, 'had a mouth like a rip in a mattress.'

The last time we saw Kyra was Labour Day weekend, Sunday morning. Dad had just come downstairs and was sitting at the kitchen table with a cup of tea, singing.

Free beer for all the workers!
Free beer for all the workers!

My brother had already showered and dressed, and was fiddling with the radio dial, trying to find the baseball score. I was still in my pyjamas, prowling deliberately around the house, thinking about school: Rachel Edwards and her sticker collection, the way my volleyball serve teetered feebly at the top of the net, the perpetual sectioning of the days.

'I think I'll make crepes,' said Mum, who had been reading the paper. She pronounced it *craypze*, then seemed to forget she had said anything at all.

There was a knock at the front door.

'I'll get it,' I called, and ran barefoot to see. I could make out a bulky, bouncing form through the stained glass. I let her in.

'Hi.' She hugged me so I couldn't breathe, my nose squashed closed, mouth full of late summer musk. I tried to relax, leaned into it. When she let go, I had to hold on to the banister until my light-headedness passed.

'Sit down,' Dad said, and poured Kyra a glass of chocolate milk.

Kyra did not sit. She tiptoed from one end of the kitchen to the other, her step light and fey, one hand wandering in the air without motive. My father, with his fondness for mimicry, was engaged.

'You know you're not supposed to be here,' said Mum, putting down the paper. 'Do your parents know what's going on?'

'Just thought I'd drop by, see how you guys are doing.' She picked up an ashtray full of nickels and fished out a tarnished watch. 'It's back-to-school time. I'm getting a new kilt and pencil crayons. I think my teacher will be a man this year, which is better. Men are much stricter. Is this a new bowl?'

'No,' said Mum, 'we've had it for a while now. Why don't you and Maddie go upstairs, and I'll make some breakfast.'

Kyra knocked a magnet into her shoulder bag as we passed the fridge.

My room was messy, the bed a nest of barely dressed dolls, half-finished origami.

'Where's Jeremy?' She pulled apart a peace crane.

'Probably outside. Who cares?'

'Not me.' She had moved on to my dresser, and was in the process of upending my jewellery box. She tugged a gold chain with a crucifix from the pile of baubles. 'Where'd you get this?'

'My mum's friend. He's Lebanese. Once he brought us a whole goat to eat.'

'Did not.'

'Did too.'

'Was it dead?'

'Duh. Of course. Could you please stop doing that? You're messing everything up.'

'I'm just looking.' She pulled a bundle of chains apart, sending a silver charm skidding across the dresser into the dark space behind.

'Kyra,' I shouted, 'you look with your eyes, not with your hands!'

'I know. I know that.'

Downstairs, Mum was making crepes, the spatula flipping them up by the edge, then over, until they were a blotchy, yellowish-tan colour, firm and eggy-tasting. Dad was jangling cutlery in one hand, and the house smelled slightly of garbage, but mostly of coffee.

'Where's your brother?' Mum asked.

'Betcha dollars to doughnuts he's in that damn shed,' Dad said. He went to fetch him.

We ate quickly. The maple syrup shone on the plates.

'Go on, might as well,' said Dad.

'Gordon,' said Mum, 'please.'

He picked up his plate and licked it clean.

'I'm leaving,' said Kyra when she was finished with hers.

'You'll make it home all right?'

'You don't have to worry about me, Reenie, I'm an independent woman.' She spun around and curtsied.

I seem to remember we sat at that table for a long time after she left, talking about the float Dad was helping to build for the Labour Day parade, the rabid squirrel Lucas had shot with his BB gun, the way summer had slumped forward into September. When the sun peaked in the sky, Mum said she supposed she should call Kyra's parents.

'That Kyra,' said Dad, 'you'd think she was King Shit of Turd Island.'

'Gordon,' said Mum, unconvincingly, 'language.'

'You're right, I'm sorry. Queen Poop of Turd Island.' He kicked me under the table.

'Dad,' said my brother, 'act your age.'

THE PRESENT PERFECT

In Montreal, people walk on rooftops. Fiona has seen them, strolling casually around brick chimneys and bubble skylights and steel vents curved like periscopes. When she first moved to the city in July, she would often sit on her small balcony with its zigzag of staircases above and below and peer out over the roofs, following the small figures as they moved across the sky, some bending to fix and check, check and fix, others simply stopping to stand, hands cupped over their eyes, as they scanned the horizon. Sometimes she was certain they were looking at her, and she would lift her hand and wave, a quick but insistent flutter, as if they had arranged to meet and were waiting, searchingly, on opposite street corners. No one had ever waved back, and this, somehow, was a comfort to Fiona, an affirmation that the roofwalkers' presence had less to do with an aimlessness of spirit than a spiritual purpose not available to her.

Fiona had left her home in Toronto because, in the space of four weeks, her boyfriend of six years had left her, her cat had died and her parents had blithely sold the family home and migrated to Florida, dragging their new hand luggage and waving their hands behind them like flightless birds. When Henry called her from work with his 'big news,' Fiona assumed it had something to do with his job as a pharmacist – a promotion or a transfer maybe – or something about one of the new queen-size mattresses they had their eye on at Sleep World, a domestic detail she could absorb and modify, then lob back at him, with a spin. She was used to this back-and-forthing; she enjoyed it, she didn't know anything else. So that when he told her he was leaving, she felt less shocked or indignant than weightless, without context. He was leaving, he said, because he had to know, he had to find out what was out there, in the world, but more importantly, within himself. Within yourself? What did it mean to look within yourself? And what could you ever hope to find there, beneath the layers, without the help of someone who had lived beside you, among your gestures and debris? But these were all questions Fiona thought of later, after Henry had boarded the plane, after her cat Mimi had staggered home, her face bleeding and broken. They were questions that surfaced fully formed in her mind, like sea monsters – palpable, if fantastic and fleeting.

Within weeks of that first phone call, Henry had sold or given away all of the furniture they agreed was his to sell, in a series of well-attended yard sales. Fiona called in sick but refused to help with the sales, instead choosing to oversee the exchanges from an upstairs window, where she sat like a trapped insect, her face butting against the screen. Henry was stupidly magnanimous in his transactions, letting certain items go for a pittance to men and women dressed in too much black and denim and silver, offering cryptic advice to eager-looking students and actually apologizing for the condition of Fiona's favourite wingback chair. He made two neat piles of the contents of the kitchen cupboards, divided the remaining curry powder into two small jars and carefully placed a stubby end of ginger root on the top of Fiona's pile where it sat, looking, Fiona thought, like a swollen chicken foot, the final ingredient in a voodoo-ish concoction.

Fiona's mother was convinced Henry was having an affair.

'There's no other reasonable explanation, Fi, it has to be a woman,' she said, cupping the back of Fiona's head against her shoulder. Fiona was crying for the first time since the breakup, long convulsive sobs that felt like sneezing or coming, that same amount of sadness and relief. They were sitting in the stark strangeness of the living room Fiona had known as a child, on two upside-down milk crates. Fiona's parents had also sold off most of their furniture, with much less psychological difficulty, she thought, than was acceptable. It seemed they had simply shrugged off the accoutrements of their past, or shed it as if it were an old itchy skin. Fiona's mother was giving her a head rub and making these back-of-the-throat noises that meant safety, that meant *There, there.* The last time she had been forced like this into the warm crook of her mother's neck, she had been sixteen, her womb scraped clean in a sterile white office.

She loved her mother for her suggestion, as much as she knew it could not be true. There was something reassuringly horrifying about the idea of Henry with another woman; she could imagine herself accusing him, brandishing a lipsticked shirt, screaming. But she knew Henry was not having an affair, and this is what scared her most. She knew that what had happened to Henry had overtaken him in the middle of the day, in broad daylight, perhaps while he was looking out the window or labelling an antibiotic. It was a transgression much more serious than any sexual betrayal, a smooth and bloodless denial of the life he had led thus far.

After the initial shock of the announcement had passed, Fiona had asked him what he was going to do. 'India,' he said. 'I'm going to India to find my path.' Fiona was prevented from outright guffawing only by the intensity of his tone. Henry had never mentioned his lack of path before, had in fact never even doubted the decisions he made in his life. It had always been Fiona who was unsure, unsettled by the haze of options that hovered around every step she took towards career, towards family. 'Easy does it,' Henry would say when she came home in tears from the advertising agency where she had worked for the past three and a half years. He would run the tips of his fingers over her back until her breathing slowed and the webs of thought reined themselves in. 'Bloom where you're planted,' her mother said when Fiona called in a panic, a series of what-ifs spilling from her mouth. And Fiona had. She had taken the man and the job and been happy. She had bloomed where she was planted.

Fiona's father was brusque, dismissive and superstitious. 'I always knew there was something funny about that guy,' he said, peeling at the plaster over the fireplace. These were the kind of comments that used to infuriate Fiona with their vague banality and absolute conviction, but today she found her father's loyalty far more comforting than her mother's rationalizations. There was nothing rational about having your heart ambushed. It was too much like something you'd watch on the evening news, shaking your head, glad you had the option of changing the channel.

The day she arrived in Montreal she had buzzed at the first brownstone apartment she saw, encouraged by the red and white *À Louer* sign in the window. Fiona had chosen Montreal because she knew the rents were reasonable, and because, from the few times she had visited, it seemed to her a comfortable place to be heartbroken.

The crowds there didn't seem to get on with it the same way they did in Toronto, and no one was looking to settle. She liked the idea that, on the country's national holiday, everyone packed up their belongings and moved. Here, instead of digging in their heels, people kicked them up. Instead of becoming resigned, Montrealers relocated and redecorated.

The concierge of the building was friendly and fatherly; he assured her that she had chosen a good neighbourhood and that the men in black coats and black hats walking the streets were not hostile.

'They wouldn't touch you if you dragged them behind a bush,' he said, and rotated his index fingers near his temples, making what Fiona at the time thought to be the sign for cuckoo but later understood, ashamedly, to be an imitation of the single ringlets of the Hasidic Jew. Later she would come to depend on the stern, knee-socked presence of the men in black – their stride so purposeful and unflinching – but at the time she had simply nodded and smiled. The apartment he showed her was large for the price, although oddly laid out, with hallways that bulged suddenly into rooms, like the body of a boa constrictor after a feeding. There was a cat lying on the windowsill.

'Shoo,' said the concierge, and pushed it down. 'It belongs to the neighbour.'

'What part of town are we in? I mean, what's this neighbourhood called?' Fiona was looking out the window at the laundromat across the street, from which two boys with orange and green mohawks were emerging, smoking and laughing. They stopped to talk to a young couple in dreadlocks. The dreadlocked man had a baby strapped to his chest. The woman was carrying a straw bag full of groceries.

'This,' the concierge stopped and pointed to his feet, 'this is Mile-End. The whole area ... ' now he waved his arms expansively,

' ... is the Plateau, the flat part after the mountain. It's very popular with the artists and the young people.'

Ah, yes. The Land of Mile-End, on the Plateau After the Mountain. This was not Canada, or even Quebec, it was the land of Narnia, Fiona thought, as the concierge led her to still another spare room.

She asked to pay month to month and the concierge agreed, somewhat reluctantly, his long eyebrow hairs skimming his eyelids. She supposed she could have signed for a year without consequence, but she still liked the feeling of impermanence it gave her to know that there were no sign-on-the-dotted-line documents to bind her, that she could find her way up to the roof one day, take one last look at the glittering cross at the top of Mount Royal, the hopeful treetops and garbage-littered laneways, and leave as she had come, with one small suitcase and a snack for the train.

In French, Fiona remembered, instead of saying 'I miss you,' you say 'Tu me manques,' or, 'You are missing from me.' This is what she practised saying to an imaginary Henry in her mirror. She thought it was probably important to say these words with a pout, or a bit of a pucker, and sometimes she perched an old army-green beret on her head for added authenticity. But out on the street she felt anything but authentic. She noticed that the women in her neighbourhood had a sort of gritty beauty about them she couldn't quite place. At times she thought it was because they sweated more profusely, or bathed less, or didn't care. Other times, she thought it had to with the fact that they wore defiant shades of mulberry and ruby lipstick to buy groceries, and left their lips daringly bare when they went out to dine. But mostly she felt inauthentic, she surmised, because she was without Henry.

Sometimes she dreamed of Henry weaving his way along the streets of Bombay, pushing through crowds, his eyes flitting from one set of facial features to another. And suddenly she too, Fiona, was in the dream, in the crowd, her eyes also searching, waiting for Henry to lock onto her gaze. Waiting for Henry to understand that, after all, Fiona was that part of himself he had been missing. Inevitably, her parents made an appearance, their faces tanned and paradoxically wrinkle-free, in the crowd of dark-skinned strangers. They wore white cotton shirts and unfettered smiles, and they had their arms linked in a kind of loose love knot.

She hadn't expected to get a job as soon as she did. She wore her best suit to the interview and made mental lists of her strengths and weaknesses on the way to the language school on the metro. Dependable, good-humoured, enthusiastic and creative teacher. Hard worker. Punctual. The manual she had at home said that your 'weaknesses' should be ruses, humble admissions of qualities your employer might actually consider strengths. 'I sometimes become overly involved in my work,' she whispered while sorting through her handbag.

Actually, Fiona had very little experience with teaching. She had once led a story-time group at a daycare she worked at in high school, and a twitchy social conscience, combined with a charismatically left-leaning university roommate, had convinced her to tutor a young offender as part of a literacy program her second year. Other than that, her only experience with a second language had been at the ad agency, where her boss, sometimes, by virtue of Fiona's high-school French, asked her to try her hand at translating copy. Fortunately, this interview turned out to be less of a test than a recruitment; ten eager candidates crowded around a conference table while an equally eager 'pedagogical advisor' tried to convince them of their suitability for the position.

Within two weeks, Fiona had four contracts, teaching on-site at various businesses around the city. The school sent her to places with names like Laval or LaSalle, rhymy places that belonged in jump-rope songs. One of her contracts was in Ile des Soeurs, or Nun's Island, a small settlement of low-rise office buildings and fresh-looking housing. The island had one strip mall, complete with a small wooden bridge that curved over a fake stream and made a satisfyingly hollow hoofy sound when Fiona walked on it to get to the washrooms. There was a special express bus she had to take to get to the island that zoomed over the water on a wide strip of highway. This was Fiona's favourite part of the journey – she felt a certain solidarity with her fellow commuters as they sat looking out over the St. Lawrence to either side, their bags clutched in their laps. She imagined they were feeling, like her, the excitement and risk of this particular ride. Fiona had never been much for history, but she thought she felt something of the arrogance and terrible naïveté of Jacques Cartier bubbling in her breast as the cold sea air rushed in through the sliding window beside her ear. This was not a voyage in increments! This bus would not stop until it got to the other side!

The groups she taught were small, and the students were, for the most part, happy to get away from their desks for an afternoon or two. They wandered in clutching company coffee cups or novelty mugs abandoned in the cupboard that read *World's Best Dad* or *Pobody's Nerfect* or *Black coffee drinkers make better lovers and I have the mug to prove it*. Fiona had once tried translating them, awkwardly, with very mixed results from her students, who seemed to think she might be making fun of them.

'The present perfect,' Fiona told her classes, 'doesn't really have an equivalent in French. It begins at a point in the past and continues up to the present, and possibly into the future. It might seem to you that because it is perfect, it's finished, an event completed, but it's not.' Fiona drew a timeline on the white shiny board using an orange magic marker. The present she marked in the middle with a scribbly dot. She hesitated before drawing another dot slightly to the left of the first one. This was the past. Then she drew an arrow in green magic marker from the second dot to the first dot, from the past to the present. 'We might say, for example, "I have eaten many bananas." In other words, up to this point, I have eaten bananas, and it's entirely possible that I may continue eating bananas in the future. We just don't know.' She drew another arrow from the present into the empty line of the future, then turned to look at the class, her face open and inviting.

Fiona was sitting at the breakfast table one morning in early August, trying to read the newspaper, when she saw a man outside her window. Her building was two storeys higher than the one next door, so that her balcony was level with the neighbouring flat-topped roof. The concierge had proudly informed her when she asked that he was also responsible for the smaller building and that there was a famous musician living in one of the larger, more expensive units. She had, on several occasions, noticed beer bottles and the soggy end of a blanket strewn across the roof. Once, there had been a pigeon nesting and cooing in a woman's high-heeled boot. Still, it surprised her, to look up at another human, at eye level, so close. She was sipping her coffee slowly, gnawing at a bagel and still considering a return to bed, when the man began pacing back and forth, peering into the windows of the apartments adjacent to hers. She stood up, tugged at the bottom of her oversized T-shirt. Who was this man? Could it be the famous musician, and, if so, why was he casing the joint? Should she confront him? She stepped onto the balcony, careful not to let the T-shirt ride up over her thighs. The man hurried over, and Fiona noticed he wore a heavy tool belt strapped around his blue-jeaned hips. Fiona had always liked tool belts for their swaggering air of usefulness. She gave a half-smile of invitation.

'Bonjour, Madame, vous habitez ce logement-là?'

She sighed. It was difficult to remain coy in a second language.

'Oui, comment est-ce que je peux vous aider?' It always seemed to her there were too many pronouns in French, or too little difference between what was plural and what was polite. She raised her eyebrows questioningly, apologetically. The man stared at her.

'You speak English?' He kicked at the edge of the roof, his thumbs hooked through his belt loops.

'Yeah.' Defeated.

'I was wondering if I could buy some water off you. I'm trying to fix the air conditioning unit and I can't hook it up from here. I mean, I could give you ten bucks.'

Fiona wasn't quite sure what he wanted her to do. She stared at his tool belt. 'Okay.'

The man pulled a hose up from behind him. It was slightly thicker than a garden hose, although it looked to be made of the same malleable rubber.

'If you could just grab a hold of this when I throw it over, I think you should be able to attach it to your sink.'

Fiona nodded and stretched out her hand.

'Actually, you better just get out of the way. I don't want to hit you.'

'Oh. All right.' Fiona moved inside. The hose flew through the air between the buildings like a snake possessed and landed on her balcony with a clank, the metal spout caught for a second between the rails. She picked it up gingerly and walked over to the sink. The spout was too big; it slipped off the faucet when she tried to screw it on.

'It's too big,' she called out to the man.

'Damn,' he said, and stomped his workbooted foot, 'I'll see if I have a washer.' He reached into his bag and pulled out a tiny silver ring. 'Here,' he gestured and drew back his hand.

He was going to throw it at her! This small, shiny, useful thing! She watched it sail through the air and stretched out her hand to catch it. The washer spun and arced, the sun glinting off its bevelled sides. The man was also watching, scratching his head and frowning at her.

She missed.

The washer spiralled down quickly and landed somewhere in the narrow strip of grass between the buildings. The man huffed and threw his arms in the air.

'Great. Now I have to go all the way downstairs to get a new one. If I have another one, that is.' He glared at her and stomped away.

Fiona watched his retreating back and bum, denim-clad and strong. 'I have missed the washer. I have missed an opportunity,' she said to the neighbour's cat, who had somehow found his way into her apartment again. The cat followed her into the bedroom and lay down on her computer keyboard.

'It's true that sometimes there is really not much difference between the simple past and the present perfect,' she explained to him when he looked at her. 'Sometimes it is more of a change in nuance than a big change in sense. It's the expectation that the action may be repeated, or, conversely, may not be repeated for a specific reason that makes the present perfect unique.' The cat blinked twice, then closed his eyes.

'Your father thinks you should come visit us, Fi. I told him you were busy with your new life – that you weren't interested in hangin' around us old people – but he thinks a vacation is a good idea. So I promised him I would mention it to you anyway. How are you? Did you get my e-mail? It's the first time I've ever used the internet – it's very cool.'

She was lounging on the futon, the neighbour's cat in her lap, a pile of workbooks on the floor next to her lamp. Fiona had been planning on doing a little marking in bed, with the help of a glass of cheap Chilean wine from the dépanneur, when the phone rang.

'Actually, I wouldn't mind a little Florida sunshine, but I'll probably wait till the weather gets worse here.' She looked out the window to Mount Royal in the distance, where the trees were still leafy and green, stalwart in the face of the rambling city that surrounded them. She imagined her parents in the shade of a broad-leafed palm tree, their lives tethered behind them like giant air balloons that had borne them up and over, to this place, this sunny beach, these lapping, lukewarm waters. 'Are you guys okay? Do you like the condo?' Fiona shoved the cat away and lay down, shrugging the phone to her ear.

'The condo's great, but your dad's going nuts with nothing to fix. You know how he is with relaxation time. Hey, honey, have you heard from Henry at all?' Her mother's question was like her wardrobe, preplanned masquerading as relaxed. Fiona lied.

'Mmm-hmm, I got a postcard. He seems to be doing really well. I guess I'll hear from him when he gets back. I think he really just needed this time on his own.'

'You're probably right. Well, we love you and miss you, here, down south. Keep on keepin' on, eh, Fi? You just gotta bloom – '

'Where you're planted. I know, Mom. Say hello to Dad for me.'

Fiona hung up the phone. The cat was asleep at her feet, making small engine noises. She rubbed his head until he began to purr.

'Le chat ronronne,' she said, and felt her tongue vibrating at the back of her throat.

Fiona was careful to start all of her classes with conversation, casually. Sometimes she talked about a current event, sometimes she took an odd or surprising fact from the back page of the *Globe and Mail*, the Social Studies feature. When the day was slow, the air stale, and she could see an eerie, computer-induced glow reflected in the eyes of her students, she revealed too much trying to lure them in, provided details of her relationship she supposed were probably best left unsaid.

'The present perfect may also be used to denote a repeated action in the past. For instance – "Henry and I have eaten at that Thai restaurant many times; the coconut milk stir-fry is really quite delicious." Or – "I have tried to get in touch with Henry several times this week through his mother, but she seems to know as little, if not less, than I do about her son's whereabouts."'

Fiona began having an affair with one of her students. He was shy and tall – an attractive, stooping combination – and he seemed to think she had cracked the code to the English language, not that it was something she grew up in, like a fish in water, but instead a series of secrets imparted to her by a mysterious superior. She did little to dispossess him of this notion. Later, she would wonder why more ESL teachers were not involved romantically with their students. It would occur to her that the makeshift set of symbols and gestures, the drawn-out syllables, the exaggerated charade – all of these attempts to be *understood* – were so very like the secret languages created and inhabited by lovers.

Henry had always told her that what he loved about her, about them, was how well they fit: the easy rocking of their lovemaking, their bodies twined together in sleep. With André, it was different, halting. He was lanky; his limbs hung off the sides of her bed. He was all splayed parts and complicated angles. Sex involved a constant and very physical reordering. After they had negotiated themselves to climax, André would fold himself up and begin his bilingual inventory of Fiona's body.

'Les lèvres – lips. Le cou – neck. Les épaules – shoulders. La clavicule – collarbone. Les seins – '

Fiona used to believe it was important, especially for women, to avoid perceiving one's body in parts. She had often told Henry she hoped he stressed the importance of holistic healing when he dealt with his customers.

'I only have about five minutes, Fi, and these are seniors we're talking about here.' Henry had been practical that way.

But when André parcelled her out the way he did, Fiona had to admit to a certain thrill, a floaty feeling at the top of her head. It was the same feeling she got sometimes at the hairdresser's, as the stylist separated and snipped, his eyes fixed on a new Fiona in the mirror, a parallel-universe Fiona, a woman Fiona could never hope to know. She supposed this was objectification.

André was from France; he had been transferred to Quebec by his software company, a large multinational whose head offices were in Chicago. Once he had mastered English he was hoping to move to the American office, but in the meantime he was happy to cook for Fiona in his small flat.

'The Québecois, they want to be their own country in the truest, bluest sense, non?' he asked her, while ladling vichyssoise into her shallow soup bowl.

'Mmm-hmm,' Fiona replied, holding the soup in her mouth for longer than necessary and noticing the complicated place setting. At home, she used a fork for everything except soup and cereal. She couldn't understand how André had so quickly acquired such a complete set of cutlery. When she had arrived at his apartment that evening, there were three sleek forks, a stolid-looking knife and a pair of spoons winking up at her from the table. André sat down, shook his napkin between her and the soup.

'Well, yes, but they still want to maintain some links to Canada.' She scraped the bottom of her soup bowl and put her spoon down, carefully, beside its mate. 'That was amazing.'

'Ah. So they are trying to kill two dead horses with one stone.' He placed a plate of coq au vin in front of her. She began to cut it tentatively, marvelling at the weight of the knife in her hand. André looked at her as though he might have asked a question.

'Not exactly.' She poured him some more wine, took a bite of chicken, rolled the sauces around on her tongue. He was still looking at her, waving the napkin in inquisitive arcs. 'It's birds, or else just one dead horse,' she began to explain, but André just smiled at her and rushed off into the kitchen to check on the crème brûlée.

One day, after an afternoon of paperwork at the language school, Fiona came home to a message from Henry on the machine. She was listening to it intently when the line beeped once, then twice quickly, the code for long distance. She imagined it was probably her mother's weekly checkup call and considered ignoring it, something she found almost impossible to do, despite the fact she knew the call would be rerouted to the answering machine.

'Fiona?'

It was Henry. Henry on hold and Henry on the line. 'How are you, Henry, are you okay?'

'I'm fine. I'm visiting this ashram near Hyderabad and I've been taking these posture workshops.' Henry was slightly breathless, and the long-distance line made his phrasing telegraphic. Declarative. Important-sounding.

'It's absolutely incredible. We do these sun salutations every morning and practise selflessness. It's great – you should really try yoga, Fiona, it's wonderfully freeing.'

Fiona had tried yoga once, when she was going through a particularly hard time at work, although it had not been at Henry's urging. She went to the classes faithfully, twice a week for three weeks, but then she missed one for some reason – a flu bug? a meeting? – and hadn't gone back. Now the only thing she remembered about them was the way the instructor used to add syllables to words, stretch them out in order to guide the class, soothingly, through the exercises. Ex-hah-ah-la-tion. Trans-feh-ehr. In-hah-ah-la-tion.

'So, when are you planning to come home, Henry?' She tried to stretch out the sounds, to keep the pleading out of her voice.

'Oh, I don't think I am – at least not for a long while. I'm trying not to plan at all, y'see. I met this guy from New Mexico – we're thinking of travelling up through the Himalayas. He knows someone in Kathmandu, and I've always wanted to see Tibet. Anyway, just thought I'd call and let you know I'm okay …'

Let her know he was okay? Fiona held the phone away from her ear, so that Henry's voice was still audible, but unintelligible, a news broadcast in a language not her own. What was most irksome to Fiona was that, in some crevice of her heart, she knew that Henry loved her, still, from across the wide and weird expanse of world. But what she could not fathom was this voice she held in her hand like something mistakenly shoplifted, this Henry-but-not-Henry. She brought the phone back up to her ear.

'Yeah, I'm glad you did, but I actually have to go. I have someone on the other line. But take good care of yourself and everything.'

'Oh, that's exactly what I'm doing. Finally taking care of myself.'

Fiona hung up the phone and sat down on the floor. The only other time she had heard Henry so high, so fast-talking, was the

night he had misfilled a prescription and had had to devise a plan
to get the drugs back before the patient took them and without
revealing that he had made a mistake. Then, she had attributed his
flushed cheeks and frantic pacing to a worry bordering on panic,
but now she wondered if he had not been thriving on the crisis.
What was it that she had missed, and how could she have missed
it? Was love believing in someone or something so completely that
it swallowed you, and you lived quite happily, never knowing you
were in the belly of the thing until suddenly you were disgorged,
unprepared, into an unfamiliar world? Or maybe not so suddenly?
Maybe, like some thick cloud, all that atmospheric affection grad-
ually, secretly, seeped away.

Some days Fiona believed she had somehow, subliminally, forced
Henry into his voyage of discovery and out of their relationship.
She was not unaware of the power of the aside, the muffled
comment, the unconscious clench (of teeth, of fists or of less obvious parts of the anatomy). She knew that, if she squinted her
mind's eye hard enough, she could come up with, if not concrete
reasons, at least diaphanous premises for his leaving. Still, she had
watched her parents squirm their way through such miscommu-
nications and emerge, if not exactly butterfly-like, at least with
some measure of grace, from the temporary cocoons they had
built for themselves.

There was only one incident that stood out in her mind as a
possible catalyst for Henry's behaviour. It was an argument – more
of a discussion, really – they had had one evening over a story
Henry had read in the paper on his way home in the subway.

'You should read this article,' he said, after she kissed him hello
at the door. He was flicking at the page and shaking his head. 'It's
so incredibly sad.' And the story was sad. A Japanese exchange

student studying in the States had been killed two nights earlier because of an unfortunate misunderstanding. He had been invited to a Halloween party and had gamely disguised himself – as Frankenstein or a superhero, Henry imagined. The story didn't say. Somehow, unwittingly, the student arrived at the wrong address, and the man who answered the door felt compelled to defend his home. He waved a gun at the student and yelled, 'Freeze!' But the student did not freeze. Instead of reaching for the sky, he had extended his hands out towards the gunman, in a gesture of pleading or prayer, or, perhaps, a half-hearted attempt at humour. A trick-or-treat in the face of terror. The parents of the student, in their grief and incomprehension, were certain their son had misheard the gunman. 'I think he must have thought the American said *please*,' they were quoted as saying.

'It's terrible, isn't it?' Henry had asked, watching her closely. 'That we can so easily mistake someone's intentions – I mean … *Freeze. Please.* It's just bizarre.'

It seemed to Fiona that Henry had missed the point. Didn't it have more to do with cultural differences, with the right to bear arms, with the rights of the individual versus the safety of the collective? And when had the Americans ever said *please*?

'Henry,' she said, 'when have the Americans ever said *please*?'

Henry stared at her, and seemed about to say something either witty or retributive, then shook his head, close-mouthed and disappointed. She had let him down somehow, had ignored the wet puppy-dog gleam in his eyes. He had thrown something long and loose and rope-like in her direction – a noose or a buoy – and she had pretended not to see it.

André took Fiona for ice cream and she told him about Henry – the phone calls, the ashrams. He listened without speaking throughout her account, squeezed her hand at all the hard parts. It was times like this Fiona understood that what she really wanted from André was not passion, or even compassion, but a sort of tender complicity – the knowledge that if she were ever arrested, the police would be on the lookout for a sidekick. Maybe it was all anybody ever wanted – someone to drive the getaway car. André asked her what kind of ice cream she was eating.

'It's vanilla, with chunks of walnuts and stuff, with chocolate fudge swirls.'

'Squirrels?' he said, and gave her a wary look.

'Oui,' she replied, 'les écureuils dans la crème glacée.' Her accent was bad, and it made him smile.

'For all intensive purpose,' he said, and looked into her eyes, 'you should be forgetting about this guy. What you need is someone to put some springs in your feet.'

Sometimes, on those hurtling bus rides across the St. Lawrence, Fiona thought she could feel her entire life around her, as if she could actually sense the whole of it, in the atmosphere, in the sky and sea to either side of the concrete bridge. It occurred to her that her birth and death were not really that far apart, and she often imagined these momentous events detachedly, as if she were watching a well-made documentary. Her death she less saw than intuited, in flashes of light on the water or the lurching of the bus as it changed lanes. It was discomfiting, to feel one's own death, but it was not frightening. It made her think of Henry and his searching, and most times it made her feel used up and a bit empty – épuisée. But what seemed more revelatory to Fiona, although she supposed they were less far-fetched, were the dream trances in which she was introduced to her beginnings. Fiona, who had never been able to remember her childhood (a fact that had prompted her to remark jokingly to friends that this was either because it was terribly traumatic or incredibly uneventful), this same Fiona could see her head crowning through her mother's vagina, scraggly and red, could feel the soft grapefruit of it in the doctor's large palm and could sense a cry straining in her lungs, like a breath, only more emphatic.

Fiona sat on her balcony one day in early October, staring out across the hydro wires and TV antennae to the red-and-gold-tipped trees at the top of the mountain and thought to herself that she did not feel lonely. 'I do not feel lonely,' she said to the neighbour cat, who was eating what looked like the remains of some old poutine on the balcony next to hers. 'I have not felt lonely for some time now.' She thought that she missed Henry a little, in the same way she sometimes ached thinking of a view she had been forced to leave behind, or the way her feet used to carry her, instinctively, to the nearest bus stop, and afterwards she could not recall exactly how she got there. But she did not feel lonely.

She was shading her eyes, straining to see the time on the clock tower three streets over, when she saw the concierge on the neighbouring roof. He was poking around with what looked like a broom handle, prodding at the tennis balls and empty Coke cans that had landed next to the miraculous mounds of grass that grew out of the gravel. She watched him for a moment, then shouted a hello, feeling a bit embarrassed and voyeuristic at not having identified herself at the first sight of him. He turned and smiled at her.

'You know, the woman who used to live here, she would grow moss up here, then use it in her artwork. It was quite beautiful, really. You do artwork?' He walked over to the edge of the roof, closer to Fiona's balcony.

'No. Well, sort of.' Lately she had taken to doodling on napkins and the backs of photocopies – swirls and spirals, small vortexes that went on forever. 'I have the rent for you – I can give it to you when you come down.' Fiona gestured towards the fire escape.

'No, no, no, you can give it to me here.' The concierge pointed to the roof and then to the distance between himself and Fiona, a deep, dark, elongated rectangle between the buildings. He extended his stick across the gap and grinned.

'Oh no, it's okay, I can give it to you when you come down.' Fiona looked down into the gap and half-shrugged an apology. The concierge began picking up bits of leftover moss and string, in the hopes, she realized, of fashioning some sort of sticky grabber for the end of his stick. 'Uh, I have Scotch tape,' she said and went inside to find her chequebook. When she came out, he was tying a pop can carefully onto one end of the stick.

'You can roll up the cheque and push it inside the hole,' he called out excitedly without looking up. But the can was too heavy and would not stay, and eventually Fiona persuaded him to extend the stick to her side as it was, without modification. She rolled the tape and fastened the cheque to the sticky spiral. The concierge drew the stick back in towards him, slowly, like a makeshift fishing pole, and retrieved the cheque from the end. Then he began to laugh. He bent his knees slightly with each gasping inhale, then held up one finger to Fiona.

'Un moment,' she whispered. It was that time of day when the sun is bent on lowering itself, a clutch of clouds at the small of its back. The air was warm and still.

'Thank you,' said the concierge, and wiped a tear from his cheek with the back of his hand.

'No problem,' Fiona replied, and looked out over the city. The rooftops spread to either side of her like rectangular lily pads.

On the neighbouring building a pigeon was pecking and preening, and, in the distance, she thought she could make out a human silhouette against the sky. She nodded politely at the figure, then watched as the sun settled, slowly, into the dark slits between them.

TROUBLE AT POW CRASH CREEK

This is how I fall asleep: there's a staircase between my throat and my brain which descends into my body. When I close my eyes I can make myself small and once I am small I can push myself down the staircase. It's important to fall but not trip. Tripping means you catch yourself – the tip of your toe, where your shoes are extraneous, too much hard point or rubber – and if you catch yourself, if you pay too much attention, you will wake up in a hard, bad way. Mostly I don't trip anymore. Not unless the day has been too big for itself, made messes at its edges that can't be tidied. If that's the case then I do tend to trip, and usually I trip a lot on those days, which of course makes me angry, and when I'm angry I just want to chew something until it bleeds. But if I don't trip I can sail down those stairs like an acrobat. Sometimes I don't even touch down. Sometimes I touch down with my hands and push off. I'm powerful and free and falling. That's the best part of the day for me, if it's a good falling.

Yesterday was my twelfth birthday and we had a brief celebration after lunch with a sugary-sweet cake from the IGA in a moulded plastic container. The cake had my name on the top in mint-green icing, as well as some blobby roses in yellow and a baseball hat in powder blue in the centre. It was my full name on the cake: RATIONAL. The short form sounds a bit Indian from India, and looks like a disease of the skin if you spell it like it sounds, like phonetics: RASH. A real short form would be RAT, I guess, which I sometimes think I would prefer and might work better with the laneway kids. I wanted to invite a couple to the party – just for diversion and diversity – but Dad said the family would suffice. The family always suffices. And Mother seemed to agree. Anyway, she wore her clever denim wraparound skirt and my favourite blouse with the purple sheen, and Dad had said to put her hair down so she did. We had tofu wieners for the meal part, which was not a big deviation since, in general, we consume them approximately four days a week. But there was also some different kind of relish and rennet-free cheese (which I believe to be slightly disgusting on the tongue but starts to taste better when you let it sit towards the back of your mouth). Because I was twelve, Mother and Dad said they had a surprise for me. I was pretty certain it would be my own gun, since every Sunday for the last year Dad has been showing me how to use his army rifle in the bathroom. We oil it and clean it and point it towards the tiles above the bathtub. Dad says, This'll get rid of all that mildew Mother's too lazy to scrub at, eh son? And we pretend-shoot, making noises like soft explosions with our mouths.

But the only present was a new CD-ROM with an advanced, interactive atlas from Mother. It was in a small, flat red package. It was obviously not a gun. And neither was the surprise. The surprise was coming next Thursday evening. Mother marked it on the calendar with a small green happy face. The surprise was a private teacher. You see, Mother and Dad have known for a long time, since I was four years old, in fact, that I am special, possibly a genius. My aptitude was revealed in a battery of IQ tests ordered from a prestigious and advanced education corporation. I am years ahead of my age group in every possible category. Off the charts, Dad said. As you can imagine, my parents were pleased with this, so they bought me a computer in order to help me develop some of my already superior skills and in order that I not feel inept with some of the new technologies that are becoming available to our society. Not that we approve of society necessarily. That's why the laneway kids were not invited. They're a good kind of accessory to the relatively fresh air and exercise the neighbourhood streets might provide. But really it's not such a good idea for me to form attachments to them.

Once I was sitting with Dad on the balcony and we saw something terrible and educational. There was a top-of-the-line BMX bike lying out in the alley. It was a beautiful work of craftsmanship. Dad and I agreed on that. Anyway, it was just lying there unattended, unheeded. Dad and I were remarking how unwise this was when a group of the laneway kids came tearing through like a bunch of hellcats. They were using a lot of inappropriate language and pushing each other needlessly. But they were laughing frequently as well, which I have to admit made me smile. I've noticed that most types of laughter, unless they're barky and fast, are contagious. Unless the laughter comes from an unpure place. The laneway kids are not exactly lily-white but they laugh like rivers are running up and out their mouths. Still, I stopped smiling because of what happened next.

One of the kids – I think his name is Sammy – picked up the BMX bike and started messing around, and I saw Dad get tense and ready. He stood up and leaned his arms on the balcony railing. The muscles in his back through his T-shirt began to twitch and roll, which is how I knew he was watching with his whole body. Sammy took the bike and rode it down to the end of the lane, then on the return trip performed five or six fairly proficient wheelies, whooping like an old-fashioned Indian (not from India). Then there was a movement from the Robertsons' back porch, which is a place we all know to avoid, due to the unsavoury nature of Mr. Robertson, and Leo, who is his socially maladjusted son. I guessed it was Leo before all the blood and afterwards we knew it was Leo because of all the blood. He came ricocheting off the porch like lightning caught in a box and fell onto Sammy while making this amplified gurgling sound at the back of his throat. I turned to go back inside. I thought maybe there was someone we should call. Oh no, son, you stay right where you are, said Dad. This is important for you to see. Dad said this without turning around. I sat back down in the same chair until he batted the railing beside him softly and I understood I was to stand at his side. Leo was punching Sammy's head. Sammy was still absurdly straddling the bike, although they had both been toppled and were lying next to the garbage bins and beer cases that form the barrier at the edge of the Robertson backyard. Sammy tried to get up, but he was pretty confused, I suppose due to the excitement of the wheelies followed by the one-two thuds of Leo's bludgeoning fists. The other laneway kids had gathered round, but at about a metre removed, since they understood Leo's violence was not limited, predictable or in any way decipherable. We all watched. When I could not watch I looked at Dad, whose eyes were narrowed like a cheetah's, trained on the cluster of kids below. When he noticed me watching him he pointed back to my lesson and nodded appraisingly.

For most of his life Dad was a soldier, which gave him a window on the world most civilians are never granted. It's a window scrubbed clean and translucent, with no rosy hue, he is fond of reminding me. It's a window that was nearly blasted all to hell when he was in the Gulf. And yet, that window, son, it's my greatest treasure. Your world view is your essence. You must polish it constantly, using all your vigilance and elbow grease. Vigilance, son, is a virtue. Vigilance is the reason we will not always be living here, in Kingston, next to the laneway and the inbreds, on the wrong side of the tracks. It is the reason why, one day, if all goes as planned, which I have every confidence it will, we will relocate to an undisclosed location and hunker in our bunker. This is one of Mother and Dad's not-so-private jokes, and it extends to and permeates all areas of their lives. Sometimes I will hear them whispering it or muttering it under their breaths, at each other or to themselves, it doesn't seem to matter. Hunker in the bunker, Mother will mumble absently while sponging off a dish, her reflection mouthing back at her in the window. And she will smile, and so will I. There is a promise in this phrase I do not fully understand, although I can feel it, like a pebble in my shoe, at all times. Vigilance, said Dad, and pointed down at the Sammy scene. Vigilance.

Leo's blows mostly connected with Sammy's head and face, but there were times his fists would land on the pavement or get tangled in the handlebars, which would draw some unkind snickers from the crowd. Dad said for me to watch the tension in Leo's neck, because when it unwound that was when Sammy might have a chance. At that point Mother came to the door and Dad said, It's nothing, just a scuffle, and she went back inside. Beside me I felt Dad leaning forward and then a sharp and slight sucking in of his breath because Leo had backed off and was standing a bit like I've seen Dad stand sometimes when his back's acting up, and once a pregnant lady at the mall. He had his feet planted about a foot apart and he was leaning back into the atmosphere with his hands bracing his body at the small of his back. It's over, said Dad, and let out a sigh. C'mon, son. He turned to go inside, expecting me to follow.

But I'll admit, I found this difficult. To Dad, I could tell, the story was over, but part of my problem as it relates to survival is that I have a problem recognizing endings – the right point to turn away. So I risked another look down at where Sammy was lying. His face was mangled and strange and unlike him. If I had to describe it or sketch it using my paintbrush program I'm certain it would end up looking like some sort of riotous field of poppies – a bit like a new screen saver I downloaded – and not like a beat-up kid at all. I believe this is one of my talents, to be able to see things in the abstract, to siphon off the beauty from a scene like Sammy. All of these thoughts and images and secret satisfactions passed through me in a second. I've noticed that about myself. I am a lightning-quick thinker, but not only this; I am able to *monitor* myself thinking. If my thoughts are the cars on a train, well, not only can I follow that train, but I'm also able to count – no, itemize – every car. I haven't yet told Mother and Dad about this since they are already more than convinced of my abilities. Besides, a person needs to keep certain things private and unobtainable, to set up quarries of important emotional and intellectual sequences, keep them safe and secret on one's hard drive.

In any case, what happened next was one of Sammy's friends came over and patted his arm, almost like you might pet a dog or a new piece of furniture in passing. And of course Sammy didn't move. I don't think Sammy was dead. I don't think that was what Dad meant. But I'll never know because that was when he grabbed me hard by the waist of my pants and hauled my nosy ass inside. I don't like not knowing the true end of things. It makes things untidy and it makes it hard at the end of the day to push myself effectively down the stairs into sleep. That night I tripped several times, then stayed unpleasantly awake listening to the animal rutting sounds from Mother and Dad's room. When sleep finally came to me it was like hands on my body, pinching and pulling, and I dreamt of black-eyed poppies and perilous, puke-making wheelies, and nothing was cohesive or pleasant at all.

But that was all before my twelfth birthday and the green happy face on the white square of the calendar: October 27th. The surprise was a teacher who would visit the apartment once or possibly twice a week, depending on how he fit the dynamic here, depending on how open he was to our particular home life, our belief systems, etc. The idea of the teacher presented a quandary for me. On one hand I was glad that Mother and Dad had finally noticed that my intellect needed, for want of a better word, some pruning. I could tell my thoughts were beginning to thrive in odd and unexpected soil. I could observe them, but I could not always predict their strange offshoots. A teacher, I was certain, could help me cope with such growing concerns. Growing Concerns. That strikes me as funny although perhaps it is not. Certainly it is only moderately clever. Still, I would like to try it out on one of the laneway kids one day if there is ever an opportunity. Or the teacher, maybe, if he is open to punning.

I'm told the teacher is currently a student at the university. Queen's University is its name, and it's purported to be one of the country's finest, although there was a night, when I was aged approximately nine and three months, when I begged to differ. We had all been awakened at 1:47 a.m., or at least that's when I remember leaving sleep, due to a disturbance at the front of the apartment building. Before I could say Jack Frost, Dad had unbolted the door and run down the stairs and out onto the sidewalk with his shotgun. Mother and I followed him, even though he kept ordering us to stay back, take cover. Our curiosity and our crankiness got the better of us. The disturbance had been caused by some purple men wearing tin cans around their waists. They were quite obviously inebriated, although at the time I didn't have the smarts or the background knowledge to ascertain this. I was terrified. They were shouting and pointing at each other, then falling in the gutters under streetlights as if to showcase their misdemeanours. Dad shot one. It was a good shot, too, but missed its mark. Not through any fault of aim, but due instead to a tin can which acted as a deflector to the bullet, making it rebound into the night and causing the purple man to remain unharmed. Scared the goddamn, silver-spooned, big-city, punk-ass bastards, though. According to Dad. Nevertheless, Queen's University does have a reputation for the formation of decent minds, and I know Mother and Dad would never choose a teacher rotten in his heart, with purple juice running down his cheeks and arms. No, my teacher would be someone with true credentials and capabilities.

The day the teacher was to arrive, Mother asked me to tidy the sitting room and I refused. This teacher, I believed, should see us as we were. Upright. Unadulterated. I did not see the point in tidying, and I felt it more pertinent to attend to my research – a new interactive amusement I had downloaded which would help me to better understand the entertainments the youth of society turn to in times of boredom and isolation. When Mother insisted, I slapped her gently on the wrist, and when she yelled at me with eyes like embers, I threw a rolled-up magazine in her direction. This was not successful, as the magazine, once airborne, unfurled and fell, without grace, to the floor. Mother unplugged the computer and watched as I squared away books and collected my sketches from the floor. Once she was satisfied, I heard her in the next room whispering to Dad. Next time I will use an eraser or a small bottle of paint. No point in mercy when there's important work to be done.

I was sitting at my computer with Jedi Fighter bleeping and flashing at me in an enjoyable way, my light sabre drawn and at the ready, when the doorbell rang. At first I was sure it must just be the water man with his squatty blue bottles, but then I put down my sword, released the mouse, mopped up my mind and understood it was the teacher who had arrived. For a moment, I'll admit, I wasn't sure where to stand or whether I should greet him formally or try to appear more relaxed. I decided to try for casual. I would learn his preferences soon enough. I heard Mother greeting the teacher in the hall. She sounded nervous and also slightly hostile, as if she wasn't sure, now the event was upon her, that she should have agreed to the teacher at all. I stepped out into the hall, casually, mind you, to make sure there wasn't going to be trouble.

The teacher is a girl! Or a lady, I suppose, although her skin looks tight and young and she was wearing some kind of shiny cosmetic product on her lips and eyes. Mother introduced us. This is Maura, Rational, she said. Then, extraneously, She's your new teacher. I nodded, then bowed ever so slightly in what I hoped was a civil, even gentlemanly, greeting. Hi there, Rational, said Maura, and actually patted me on the shoulder. Mother said she would show Maura around, and then we could start our lesson in the computer room. Then the two of them shoved off, as Dad would say, two ships down the hallway. Well, I thought, she appears to be friendly. Whether she is at all bright still remains to be seen. I did not open up the Jedi program again, since I would not want her to enter while I am playing and assume I am in some way frivolous and uncommitted. I sat at my desk with the mathematics textbook in front of me and made some fascinating patterns with the pencil shavings I had piled to the side. The shavings were perfect, curled and crisp, and I enjoyed the way I could fit one snugly on each finger. The black dust, too, afforded some distraction. It smudged and stained the skin of my palms so the lifelines darkened ominously. When Maura finally entered the room, my hands were black with lead, and I found I could not stop staring at her nipples. She wore a relatively flimsy T-shirt in a pale peach colour, with a black cardigan overtop, and the nipples themselves seemed to be straining both out and inwards, like the eyes of an old gozzy cat. In the weeks to come I would learn that the pale peach T-shirt was in fact an anomaly. Usually Maura wore only dark colours, and only once did I see her wearing a skirt. It seemed to me she must be an emotional yet reserved young woman.

All right, Maura said. Where shall we sit? I stared at her. Mother too seemed shocked. What we were looking for was direction and assurance, and this perky rise of a question gave us neither. I decided it was up to me to take charge. I wheeled my computer chair slowly and deliberately over to the other desk, then swivelled it to face the mathematics textbook, then around again so that the seat was open and accessible. Beckoning, even. Could I have made myself any more clear? Apparently so. Maura shrugged and smiled. I see, you want me to sit there? I nodded and lifted my hands to show their state and the obvious need for me to wash them clean. Oh, were you outside? she asked brightly. I shook my head no, and scurried off. This was a girl who seemed to see an opportunity for conversation everywhere. I would have to be careful.

When I came back from the bathroom, hands clean and attitude keen, Maura had settled herself in the chair I suggested. This pleased me. Well, she said, when I sat down next to her, I suppose we should begin. She said this with a grin I thought better suited to the laneway boys than a university student, but I decided I would bear with her policies until I got a better handle on her approach. I suppose so, I said, and attempted a grin in return.

I always like to start these sessions with a bit of 'get to know you,' so let's begin with a little adjective game? And there it was again, the jaunty uplift at the end of her sentence. I stared at her. She nodded. In assent to what? I thought.

Maura continued. How it works is we come up with words to describe ourselves, only the trick is to find a word that begins with the same letter as your name. For instance, I'm Maura, so my adjective could be morose, or militant, or malevolent. She looked at me and I smiled despite myself, and saw victory in her eyes. Of course I'm none of those, but I suppose I could be if you refuse to do your homework. She glowered prettily and lost me completely. Where was all of this going? Mother had said a Math Teacher. Mathematics Maura. Instead I was lumbered with some pointy-nippled, alliterative clown. I waited for her to tell me something I did not already know. She was looking at me, then over at my computer, around which I had taped some of my favourite sayings and illustrations, clipped from *Canadian Geographic* and some of Dad's old *Reader's Digest*s. Some were jokes, and I could tell she was calculating how to use these as a point of entry. Runty, I said. Relaxed. Reticent. Rheumatoid. Runny-nosed. And, finally, Rennet-free. Yes, she said. Then, Rennet-free. Then, I see. Then, Well then. We stared hard at each other and I perceived her registering *something* about me – the extent and dynamism of my mind, the latitude and longitude and absolute loopedy-loop of my mind. How it *moved*, my mind.

Maura opened the mathematics textbook. Well, she said again. Since you haven't yet had any formal training in math, I thought we'd start with something simple, and then we can build from there? I could see this was becoming a trend. I was forced to agree with what was essentially not my choice at all in order for her to proceed.

That day the topic was fractions, and I'll admit that I stumbled through. I could not help but see the dividing lines as small see-sawing platforms upon which the numerator balanced precariously above the denominator. A number that nimble had to be more powerful than the one below, and yet this was not the case at all. In fact, according to Mathematics Maura, the bottom number was King, the royal container for the top number. How could this be? It did not make sense, visually or otherwise. I began to obsess over Maura's collarbones, which peeked like lovely smooth twigs out of the top of her T-shirt. It was impossible for me to concentrate on the questions for the final quarter-hour. I began to play with pencil shavings and twice I noticed the upswing fade from Maura's voice as she pointed at my paper, then back at the text, as if the simple line she'd drawn in the air would somehow link my thoughts. I will admit also to a great sense of relief when it was finally time for her to leave.

Mother stood with Dad in the doorway like a picture in a frame. They looked solid, I thought, respectable, if modest, possibly shabby. This was the first Maura had seen of Dad, but if she was at all shocked at his presence she didn't show it. She stood up quickly and extended her hand. Hello, Mr. Raconteur, she said, and I started. It wasn't often I heard him addressed this way. Even Mother calls him Dad. Hello, young lady, said Dad. And how's our young man? He's doing very well, said Maura smoothly, for the first day. Liar, I thought, but smiled agreeably at Dad because of those collarbones. Well, I suppose Mother has given you the tour, said Dad and waved his hand behind him. Maura looked momentarily baffled, then nodded. Next time you'll have to stay for tea – herbal, of course. That would be great, said Maura, but I could sense an impatience in her, and something else – panic? – ruffling her exquisite girl-feathers.

So, off she went, my Mathematics Maura, to whatever sphere it is she occupies outside of this, my home, which for us will suffice. Which will always suffice. Allow me to tell you something about the place I live. Kingston, Ontario, is a university and prison town, with a population of approximately 112,000, not including the prisoners, whose number, as you may surmise, tends to fluctuate according to sins and sentences and certain surprises involving spades and wire cutters. The home we occupy, although it suffices, is nevertheless located, as I mentioned, on what most people would no doubt refer to as the wrong side of the tracks. Which means our yards are gravelly, rife with weeds as tough as nails, of which there are a preponderance as well, rusty ones at that. Which means quite a number of my grown neighbours spend their days, as Dad has explained, banging on their own goddamn thumbs in factories and banging on their wives at night. Their women are blowsy with poufed-up hair and terry-cloth short shorts. Skanky, says Dad. Slovenly, says Mother. They are all, according to Mother and Dad, uneducated, with minds amputated through neglect and bad breeding. Nevertheless, we choose to live here due to economics and humility. Mother has a small job out at the department store, where she mostly stays in the stockroom at the back sorting merchandise as Dad's not keen on her having a great deal of interaction with the general public. Or the great unwashed, as he has dubbed them. So our income is modest – Mother's part-time paycheque and Dad's military pension, plus the compensation for the fact that he came home a bit fucked up (his words). Still, we won't be here long. Once we are prepared and our route is secure, we will pack up and depart for the bunker, but until then, it is important for me to continue with my studies, to arm myself with knowledge, to ensure my grey matter remains engorged and engaged. And so Maura continues her visits. Every Thursday I anticipate her steps up the stairs to the corridor, the thump of her hiking boots, the swish of her knapsack against the wall as she rounds a corner.

The last time Maura was here, we became more intimate in our conversation, due to the fact that I was not acting the model student. The previous night had been fractured, a throwback to the days of my youth when the stripy men invaded my dreams, climbing in clumsily, with crowbars, wrecking my world view. When I was a child of three, articulate in speech yet not versed in the ways of the world, I tried to explain my dreams to Mother and Dad. I told them of the lone, long-armed prisoner, rowing his way across Lake Ontario, a lantern perched on the wooden strut in front of him, his eyes fixed on his destination, and his destination me. Goddamn, said Father, three years old and already the kid's got a soldier's instincts. With dreams like that, son, it's mind power you gotta use. You just focus your mentalities in the same way that piece of crud is pointing his lantern. You repel him with your mind. And if that doesn't work, well, you come fetch me and I'll fetch my rifle. This was Dad's well-reasoned advice and for the most part it was effective. I'd push myself down the sleep stairs and when the light began to grow closer, when those long arms reached like live wires out of the darkness, I focused and repelled. Even when Long Arms was able to reach Mother in the daytime hours, leaving blue marks like bunny paw prints, like mud stains, on her soft arms and cheeks, even then, in the nights, I could sharpen and shoot with my very own mind.

But the night before the intimate conversation with Maura, Long Arms had returned, with a new tactic. This time Long Arms wore a suit and carried a newfangled laptop. On his laptop he was able to design and animate virtual handcuffs which floated from the screen and onto my wrists, then glasses that detached from the monitor, fused to my face and blurred my sight. I screamed but it made no sound. Lightning lacerated the thick night sky. I did not sleep. Consequently, my attention span during the lesson with Maura was shortened, and when she was forced to dissect a word problem with me for the fourth time, with no discernible result, she rolled the pencil into the crevasse of the open math text and turned towards me. Raconteur, that's quite a name you have there. Related to some far-off monarch or coureur de bois? I shrugged. It's possible, I said. We live in a country of displaced descendants. True, she said. Is your father from Quebec? His grandfather came over from France with Cartier, I asserted boldly. Cartier? Maura said. Rational, do the math. I raised my eyebrows and she sighed. Do you speak French? Oui, I said, un peu. But it won't be necessary anyway. What do you mean? When we move, I whispered. Where are you moving to? There was a renewed brightness in her tone. She was interested in me. I described the bunker as I saw it: a slope-roofed building made of cedar planks whose bulk was buried beneath the ground. Its solar panels were huge and spotless, gleaming with potential energy. The front door opened with a sound like the entrance to a spaceship or the lid of a jam jar. A tried-and-true fuh-wup. The stairs leading down to the living area have a railing that resembles a strong birch-tree branch, and there are portals along the way for storage and respite. My room is near the front of the house. It has low ceilings and cool dark corners and a set of triple-decker beds. A computer station, of course, and a brother. A brother, eh? Yes, I said – and, without meaning to – to fight against Long Arms. Maura leaned in close and jostled the textbook with her elbow. Who's Long Arms? Oh, just a character from a computer game, I replied breezily, but under the desk my thighs had begun to tremble.

I had broken one of my own rules – to never ever let Long Arms, or anyone else who tripped me on the way down my stairs, clamber up and into the broad light of day. Long Arms deserved incarceration. His freedom spelled definitive disaster for all. Well, said Maura, you'll have to show me the game one day. Sounds like a true villain. I nodded and she wrote some homework for me at the top of a blank page. Homework, I said. She nodded. For the home-schooled, I added, in case she was somehow, miraculously, unfamiliar with sarcasm. She squeezed my shoulder and got up to leave. You got a middle name, Rational? Yes, I replied. Joseph. Huh, Maura said, and for once I could not detect the mild, artificial inquisitiveness that so often characterized her repartee. Joe, eh? Well, see ya next week. Yes, I said, next week.

I switched on the computer, but turned down the volume so I could hear Maura sliding her feet into her boots and grunting delicately as she bent to lace them up. Then there was a gasp and an obviously unplanned-for step backwards. I slid from my chair and padded over to investigate the hallway scenario. From my position in the doorway I could see Maura's cardigan-clad back, and through tactics Dad had apprised me of, I sensed her nervousness in the way her vertebrae seemed stacked slightly askew. Mr. Raconteur, I heard her say in a tentative, non-Maura voice. I craned my head around the corner, risking discovery. There was something interesting about to unfold. The foyer of our apartment is crowded, to say the least, as we have been stockpiling supplies the length of my lifetime; it was when I pushed my caul out into the raw, unchecked world that Mother and Dad truly understood the value of Hunker in the Bunker. The hallway is also a repository for the Bottle People – smooth, see-through blue dwarves delivered every Thursday (Maura Day!), then collected the following Tuesday when they have been drained. They are awkward and unwieldy and harmless, but god knows we could never trust what comes gushing out of the goddamn government-sanctioned taps. So, for a moment I could not see Dad, or I could see only his arm, which dangled loose like a noodle by his side, then bent to link to his other arm behind his back. At ease. But when I tilted my head slightly to the left, I understood Maura's distress. Dad was naked. Buck. And at ease. Maura took a step forward, then another step back. Dad's eyes were glazed and yellowish like custard and I could tell he was having difficulty focusing.

The tragic thing about Dad is that the Gulf War gave him a syndrome, simultaneously clearing and clouding his world view. Consequently, there are days when the chronic fatigue, in combination with the side effects from the Ativan, coerce him into a feisty forgetfulness. This day, a Thursday, a Maura Day, he had forgotten to dress himself, and it can't have been an agreeable sight for my Maura. You see, Dad is no spring chicken, and although his body is taut in places from the extensive training he's undergone, in others it appears strangely stuffed, and in still others – his groin for example – slack and overused. I don't mind saying the sight of it terrified me. Not for myself, or my Dad, but for Maura. I was scared she might not understand. I was scared she would never come back. Fortunately, Dad didn't speak. In fact, Dad didn't even seem to notice Maura. He swayed slightly on the spot, then turned and marched like the soldier he was back into the bathroom, where I heard him pissing into the bathtub, mumbling Shit, shower, shave under his breath. As for Maura, she was not long for the foyer. I watched her clutch her bag to her chest and charge out the door. I could only hope she didn't scare easy.

The Day of the Trouble at Pow Crash Creek was a Tuesday, and I would put the time at approximately 2:37 p.m., although I may be out by a margin of three to five minutes. Mother, Dad and I had just finished a late lunch of frozen peas, meatless baloney and unripe tomatoes from the balcony, and were digesting quietly around the kitchen table. It was one of Dad's off days, so Mother and I were both glad of the post-meal lull. Dad closed his eyes, pushed out his solid stomach and belched. Hunker in the bunker, he said in the breath at the tail end of the burp. Hunker in the bunker, Mother and I agreed, but with our eyes only. Then Dad heaved himself away from the table and stood unsteadily. He was wearing the T-shirt Mother had brought him from work with the orange piping and large North Carolina decal, his blue-and-white-striped pyjama bottoms and a housecoat with a camouflage-type pattern. His feet were bare, his toenails tough and untamed, like those of a rhinoceros. Mother and I sat still, gauging the atmosphere. Mother, Dad said, could I talk to you in the parlour? Mother nodded, and I sank in my chair, relieved. Whatever it was that was chafing at Dad seemed to be unrelated to me and my goings-on. I sighed, then downed some apple juice, yearning for Maura. There were mutterings from the front room, the parlour, the sound of furniture being dragged across the floor – from the velocity and volume of the noise, I surmised it must be the sofa – and then more mutterings. Mother or Dad? I could not tell. I smoothed my hair down on my head and arranged my cutlery on my plate in preparation for the day that was laid out before me.

I looked out across the table to the sink, and above the sink, past the curtains, to the sky. The sky was blue and one fat cloud sat in its centre like a toad. I thought I would ask permission for a period of play in the laneway that afternoon. Just me and the laneway kids under the sky. That, I thought, I can quite easily foresee in my afternoon. I hummed the theme from Jedi Fighter to myself and traced the contours of the toad cloud onto the placemat with my fork. Then there was a sound I can only describe as an upper-case POW from the parlour, followed by a CRASH. I froze like a scared rabbit. I was silent like a snake, considering. Long Arms, I concluded, and hurried to fetch Dad's rifle. But when I ran out into the hallway, Dad was already there, rifle in hand. Son, he said. And nodded. Then he padded into his and Mother's bedroom, leaving me to assemble the chunks of story left behind.

Mother was lying on the floor in the parlour next to the sofa, which was also lying on its side. It was obvious to me that Long Arms had harmed her, but I could not at the moment locate the source of the hurt. I had a first-aid manual Dad had passed on to me for my ninth birthday, and its lessons came into stark effect at that very moment. I circled the area around Mother, checking for hazards, checking for clues. No fire, no wire, no glass, no gas, no bee, no danger to me or the victim. The area was clear, save some pencil shavings and a shopping receipt that may or may not have slipped from Mother's pocket as she fell. I stowed the receipt in the waistband of my pants for further investigation, then dropped into a crouch and waddled forward towards Mother's head. She was breathing. I could feel the soft spurts of air coming from her nostrils. I dropped then to my knees and bent to lift her arm. It occurred to me that I had never actually seen Mother's inner arms before – the one I held in my hand was pale, the blue lines like ghostly misplaced watercolour brushstrokes. It occurred to me that I should one day paint this curious innocent inner arm. It occurred to me that I was staring Art in its face. I traced the vein down to Mother's wrist and pressed my index and middle fingers down gently, feeling for a pulse I took for granted, given her regular, relaxed breathing. The blood jumped like tiny toads in a sac under my fingers, and made my mind jump back to the cloud toad in the sky. I don't often put much stock in signs, but this seemed irrefutable. I turned Mother over to look into her face and that's when I saw the purple squatting toad on the side of her head. She had not been shot, as I had earlier feared, but instead clubbed, and by the markings of the wound, by a gun's heavy barrel. There was a small trickle of blood running down her cheek like a tear. I lay down beside her and placed her wrist with its watercolours and active toads across my chest. I stared at the trickle, which ran down the toad-shaped mound like a creek down a mountainside.

Pow Crash Creek, I said out loud, and placed one of my fingers to the blood, then licked at it quickly.

When I first got my computer, I spent a good deal of time performing searches on the internet. Mostly I searched the city of Kingston, Ontario, my city, because I suppose it excited me that the city itself was actually known. It thrilled me that outside people knew it existed. Come see what Kingston has to offer! one of the sites trumpeted, and for weeks whenever I wanted Mother or Dad's attention, I would repeat this line. I propped myself up and repeated it now to Mother. Come see what Kingston has to offer! I whispered it in her ear. When she didn't respond, I spoke aloud. Hunker in the Bunker. Then, Long Arms Versus the World. Then, Trouble at Pow Crash Creek. When she still didn't respond, I began to cry, unmanly tears that squirted out of my eyes and onto the toad squatting on Mother's muddled face. I began to wait for Maura.

I have been writing all of this down at the back of my yellow mathematics notebook, writing towards the middle, towards the beginning, so that I suppose, eventually, the squiggly stubborn numbers and the squiggly supine letters will meet in some confused entanglement, or simply stop, fade into each other. In any case, on this day, the day of Pow Crash Creek, I have decided to write my name on the inside cover. I suppose I always thought it would be a good idea to remain anonymous, in case Mother or Dad were ever to come upon the notebook. I could then affect ignorance and denial. Pretend some laneway lunatic had snuck up the drainpipe to channel my spirit. But now I think it might be important for those on the outside to know exactly who I am if ever the book goes missing in action, so to speak. Especially since the next time Maura comes here, I am not letting her leave alone. I will walk down the stairs, by her side, past the stacks of paperbacks and crowds of toilet-paper rolls, my mathematics textbook tucked beneath my arm, and – to the best of my knowledge – I will keep on walking. So here I am going to write my full name: Rational Raconteur. A name not without a gloss of irony if you have some feel for the French, which I do. Nevertheless, a name only. A receptacle for spirit and intellect, and in no way an indicator of the person I will one day become.

ACKNOWLEDGEMENTS

This book is in memory of my father, who would have been proud of me had I never written it. For my mother, who is proud of me because I did. And for my sister, who never stopped believing that I would.

Many people and places helped this collection through its growing pains. I would like to express my gratitude to the Toronto Arts Council, the Ontario Arts Council, the Canada Council for the Arts, the MacDowell Colony, Fundación Valparaíso, the Humber School for Writers and Concordia University, all of whom helped me find time and space to work. Some of these stories appeared in slightly different form in the following publications: *Prism international, Matrix, Descant, the Journey Prize Anthology* and the anthology *She Writes*. Thank you to their editors for supporting my writing in its beginning stages.

Bev Burke, Joan Firmin and Lara Edwards provided storage space, mending, legal advice and much more. Dan Goldman taught me the meaning of *machaya*. Carolyn Burke and Sue Merrill had bucket loads of faith. Joel Freeman gave generously of his time and design talent. Catherine Bush played midwife to some of my first scrawlings. Susan Kernohan was a firm and forgiving friend and editor. And the kind and unflappable Alana Wilcox eased me through the journey from manuscript to book.

Finally, all my love and thanks to the inimitable, irrepressible Charles Checketts, who always makes me laugh – especially when things aren't very funny.

ABOUT THE AUTHOR

Heather Birrell's short fiction has appeared in *Prism international*, *The New Quarterly, Descant, Matrix, The Journey Prize Anthology 13* and *She Writes*. She is a fellow of two writer's residency programs, Fundación Valparaíso in Spain and the MacDowell Colony in the US, and the recipient of Concordia University's David McKeen Award for best creative writing thesis. A teacher and traveller, she currently lives in Toronto with her partner Charles Checketts.

Typeset in Sabon Next and printed and bound at
the Coach House on bpNichol Lane, 2004.

Edited and designed by Alana Wilcox
Cover design by Rick/Simon
Cover idea by Joel Freeman
Cover image by Charles Checketts, courtesy of the artist
Interior drawings by Charles Checketts

Coach House Books
401 Huron Street (rear) on bpNichol Lane
Toronto, Ontario
M5S 2G5

416 979 2217
1 800 367 6360

www.chbooks.com
mail@chbooks.com